MW01128608

TRY THE NEW CANDY

ARON BEAUREGARD

<u>WARNING</u>
This book contains scenes and subject matter
that are disgusting and disturbing, easily
offended people are not the intended audience.

JOIN MY MAGGOT MAILING LIST NOW
FOR EXCLUSIVE OFFERS AND UPDATES
BY EMAILING
AronBeauregardHorror@gmail.com

WWW.EVILEXAMINED.COM

DEADICATION

This book is dedicated to my family who has always believed in me and supported me, Katie, Mom, Ron, Beau, Sheila, and Kenny.

Also thank you to Jean, Daddi Bace, Day Day, Mike from Reel Judgements, Steady Eddy, Ronix, John the Skeptic, Austin the Starving Artist, John the Aviator, Silent Sarita, Jimmy Towner, and both Lil & Big Jorge.

"One man's pornography is another man's theology."

- Clive Barker

TRY THE NEW CANDY

Stanley was finally on the home stretch, only a few miles out from the office on what felt like an endless trail of asphalt. Working in the vending business sounded easy enough, but in truth, it was an especially tasking and tedious occupation.

He was a hand-selected jack-of-all-trades. His list of responsibilities included managing the inventory and tracking purchases, loading the truck, and traveling to all vending locations to execute the restocking. Not to mention, he was also in charge of emptying money, wrapping the coins, counting the cash, and making the bank deposits.

The gig was extremely lonesome, draining, and unrewarding, both psychologically and fiscally. Stanley didn't exactly have some sparkling future that he was looking forward to or any sort of promise at all really.

He came out of high school diploma-less and entered the job market at the age of seventeen. He met his current boss and owner of The Snack Express, Red, not too long after he'd dropped out.

He'd become intrigued by a flyer he noticed hanging on some cork-board near the exit at one of the local supermarkets. It had nice flashy colors and forecasted a lucrative, stable potential career option, regardless of the prospective employee's educational background. This instantaneously grabbed Stanley's attention, it was exactly the sort of sign he longed for.

Finally, a position that suited him to a tee. He went home later that evening and reviewed the information on the ad once again before working up the nerve to finally dial the number.

The phone rang, leaving Stanley in a suspended state of anticipation, his finger nervously toying with the phone cord. He was more than ready for his life to become closer to the happy man in the picture that sat partially crinkled in his moist palm.

Red answered the line with a commanding but professional tone that immediately filled Stanley with a skittish sensation. He embodied a boldness in his articulation that oozed certainty and an inflexible confidence.

After talking with Stanley for just a few minutes, it wasn't difficult for Red to comprehend that the boy he was dealing with wasn't working with a full deck of cards. He'd known his fair share of nitwits throughout his colorful existence, so it wasn't hard for him to sniff out a slow one.

Most employers might see this as a detriment to a potential candidate, but to Red, one man's trash was another man's treasure. In fact, if he exploited Stanley strategically, he was a goldmine. The boy who had called was precisely the young soul he was seeking. He set up a meeting with him for the following evening.

Stanley was more anxious than he'd ever been while

pacing outside the office waiting for Red. His actions gave an appearance that seemed like he was about to be put in the electric chair, opposite of being given a life-altering opportunity. His palms again grew sweaty and he'd come down with a slight shiver that had nothing to do with the temperature.

Red arrived a few minutes later than he'd said he would and welcomed him. As Stanley stepped inside, he was mesmerized by the small office. It was so cozy and clean, unlike his house.

Red's desk and furniture bled a regal character into their surroundings that any young professional would kill for. He had one rather unique item standing against the wall opposite his office door. It was positioned strategically to flaunt and bombard folks with his success and grandeur right as they entered.

There it sat, a custom gold-plated vending machine, pimped out to the max in the gaudiest of presentations. It was in mint condition, the state-of-the-art digital keypad and readout looked virgin, just there to impress. And that it did, it looked like it cost tens of thousands. In all likelihood, it was probably little more than a normal machine, gorgeous in a cubic zirconia kind of way but essentially just a braggadocios showpiece.

Red offered him a seat in the leather chair in front of his desk and they both took a load off. It was there that Red briefed Stanley on what the job would entail. It was basically work that anyone could do after some remedial instruction and a few rounds of repetition.

Precisely like the ad said, essentially all he needed was a warm body. Red explained the ins and outs of the business to him, all of which he was very receptive to and, within a matter of weeks, Stanley was running routes all by himself.

For the first time, he was good at something and it came to him almost effortlessly. Some people were destined to create technology, provoke philosophy, or even leave a legacy by innovating humanity. Stanley's destiny was to make sure those people had a selection of sweet or salty treats (their choice) when they went on break.

Red, never being one to miss a window at getting a bigger bang for his buck, intentionally left out a revealing truth. The number of routes that Stanley was expected to run equated to the work of about one and a half people. On a bad week, maybe two.

The amount that Stanley was earning was far less than what the workload called for. In the beginning, he didn't see an issue. Though after fielding a few holiday dinner questions from family, Stanley was publicly made a fool of.

The embarrassment felt hot on his face as he realized his compensation had been tied to his competence. His cousin, like himself, was doing entry-level work, except poor Stanley had been stuck working almost double his hours and making just a pinch more.

His pride aside (which was something he'd never been particularly high on), he knew things could be much worse for a man of his capacity. He made enough to survive on and had even managed to snag a place of his own, but his earnings didn't leave much wiggle room or time to pursue any passions.

One of Stanley's favorite pastimes was watching professional wrestling. To him, it was legit. Many of his isolated evenings prior to his employment under Red were spent screaming words of encouragement at the television when his favorite wrestler, Madman Moses, graced the screen. Unfortunately, due to his time-guzzling schedule as of late, he didn't even know if Madman had the championship belt anymore. This understanding left a sadness in the pit of his potbelly like few other things could.

Stanley was a dummy, but he wasn't dumb enough to not realize it. So many people had been kind enough to highlight his ineptitude for him over the years. This awareness stood firmly. In addition, a cross-pollination of enlightenment had occurred, making him finally register that the world could be a cruel place at times and offered little pity to the pitiful. On the contrary, they found joy in mocking him and pointing out his challenges with understanding things that were seen by the masses as common sense.

He hated those words. "Common sense." It was a term that was not relative to him but something that everyone else was equipped with naturally. In part, it was why the job was a perfect fit for him, he didn't have to deal with other people, just machines. Even if he worked like a dog and was being taken advantage of while his employer reaped the benefits, it was probably better than the alternative.

What could he do exactly? Go and work at a grocery store and be forced to integrate into the social structures that those sorts of places promoted?

He couldn't do that again; it was just like high school where his lack of intellect and non-existent communication skills had driven him into depression prior to throwing in the towel. He'd accepted that he would be wandering through life impoverished and mindless at this point. At least in his current situation he could do so in isolation.

He found himself strangely comfortable with that dark concept until one seemingly ordinary afternoon when some light was shed upon it. It was just prior to his fifteen-year anniversary when Red's attitude began to morph unexpectedly.

By now, he'd become accustomed to The Snack Express's crude business cycle, this style of rotten repetition, and his blunt dealings with the old man. Based on the history he'd tolerated, at this stage, any mutation would be a welcome one.

Red called Stanley into his office for a meeting and closed the door behind him. He narrowed his eyes in Stanley's direction while taking the seat behind his desk. Stanley assumed this was the old annual speech where Red would inform him that his rate could not be increased.

After supplying Stanley with a buffet of gripes and issues that would complicate any wage-hike, Red usually had a highly entertaining excuse—something that was an obvious lie.

Like last year, he'd complained about tax revisions the state had passed on small businesses being a bone of contention. Apparently, these amendments were what was making things tight. Not quite as tight as the BMW Red pulled up in that morning, but close.

"You wanted to see me, sir?" Stanley asked earnestly.

"Yes, Stanley. I wanted to bring you in today to celebrate your fifteen-year anniversary. Even though this company only consists of the two of us, you deserve to be recognized."

Stanley was shocked, genuinely taken aback by the kind remarks. He'd never breathed anything like this before, in fact, Red never even acknowledged that an anniversary was a thing until that moment.

Maybe after all of these thankless years of Stanley allowing himself to be taken advantage of, Red had finally found it in his heart to give him a raise. He was too stunned to do anything but remain speechless as Red continued.

"In the fifteen years you've been here, you've never once been late, you've never missed a route, and you've never complained. You've constantly put the business ahead of your own needs allowing for us to both succeed. Most importantly though, the accounting has always checked out. On a job where you've constantly been surrounded by coins and cash, you've never taken a cent from me, Stanley."

Red rose up from behind his desk and took a step toward the window behind him, looking outside.

"No, sir, Mr—" Stanley began concurring with Red before being cut short.

"I have ten years left, Stanley. Ten years until my complete, full-on retirement. After that, I plan to be somewhere further down south and riding out the rest of my days poolside. When that day comes, I want to do something for you." He turned back from the window now to face Stanley.

"The machines on our routes don't so much matter as much as the locations do. When I started this business, I was able to use my savviness and salesmanship to secure us the highest-trafficked, most ideal sites to seed our vending machines. A few decades later, we've blossomed, obviously due to my strategy and, to some extent, your consistency. What I'm telling you is that I don't have a child, Stanley. I could just cash out and sell the machines and the routes when I'm done, but instead, I plan to hand it off to you."

"Oh, Mr. Campbell, you're… you're such a good man. I can't believe this!" Stanley exclaimed, sounding like a child that had just seen his favorite magic trick.

"Now, settle down a minute, Stanley. This is how it's going to work. We both know you can do everything to run this company, you know it inside and out. I plan to sell it to you at a modest price of ten thousand dollars, although it's probably worth double that. Think of it as an appreciation for your years of outstanding performance, kind of like a big raise all at once. Immediately, once you've taken over, you'll notice a substantial increase in your paycheck. You'll be able to buy many nice things in addition to making your monthly payment to me. After about a year of operations, you'll have already paid me off. Then you're looking at some real play money, mister. Once you've reached that point, then it will be time for you to find your own, Stanley. Give someone an opportunity like I gave you."

Stanley found himself attempting to hold back his tears, unable to respond after listening to Red's heartfelt speech. It began to slowly dawn on him that now he would no longer be doomed to work to the bone until the day he croaked.

He could now have a future like normal people did, maybe he could find a hobby to extract some joy in his days. See some wrestling events and keep closer tabs on the careers of his favorites like Madman Moses.

"What do you say, son?" Red smiled, extending his hand toward him.

Stanley continued to sniffle as he accepted the handshake and nodded his head. There was no way he could ever repay Red for injecting a smidgen of meaning into his life. Things were finally set to change.

Apparently, the sun does shine on a dog's ass once in a while.

🝙 🝙 🝙

The next eight years went by without a hitch, Stanley and Red were chummier than ever. The labor continued to get done in an impeccable fashion, just as it did previously. Now, Stanley put even more attention toward his already flawless work ethic, understanding that he was working for a later version of himself.

As money continued to roll in, Red began to make his arrangements. At times, he'd even ask Stanley his opinions on different parts of Florida and some of the condos he had his eye on. Everything was going according to plan, until one day someone else showed up at The Snack Express.

Her name was Candy and she was built in a way where there couldn't have been a more applicable name selected for her. She had the vintage sort of air-headed bombshell look, the likes of Anna Nicole Smith. The first time he'd seen her, she was in Red's office, bending forward over the desk as Stanley entered, clenching a deposit slip.

Both Candy and Red's mouths were open and salivating, tongues coiled around each other like two knotted snakes. Candy's tits projected so far out that they pushed her sweater forward to absurd lengths, causing the bottom of her top to hike up. This helped to showcase her eye-catching, dangly navel ring that was cinched in near her finely sculpted abs.

This didn't feel good to Stanley. Red's attitude had finally changed toward him, not that he was some peachy saint now, but he had certainly grown cordial.

After years and years of loyalty and sweat, he was supposed to get his due now.

He was supposed to get what was only fair after swallowing the sacrifice and being paid fucking peanuts for his entire existence. He could sense that was all in jeopardy now because the bitch had her hands down his pants.

Stanley had zero doubt; he might have been as slow as a crockpot, but he understood exactly what was going on. He recognized the way that she looked at him. Drooling venom with a disgusted heartlessness trapped in her eyes. It was like something out of the movies he'd seen on his television at home.

He knew she thought he was a fucking bug and she seemed the type that had no problem swatting a fly or crushing a cockroach. Stanley avoided eye contact and dropped the deposit slip on the old man's desk.

After their awkward initial encounter, it didn't take her long to have a talk with Stanley. He was loading the bags of chips and chocolate bars into the truck when she approached him.

"Listen up, retard," she commanded in a dead cold tone. "Red told me his plans for The Snack Express but I want you to rest assured those are going to change soon. I know you've been kissing the old man's ass for a while now but all the years you've been sucking up can be forgotten with just a few minutes of my sucking up." She licked her lips seductively.

Stanley stared into her sparkling eyes with a hatred that didn't come easy, a loathing that was difficult to digest, something that he hadn't felt for anyone else. Not even the people who called him names or drove him out of high school. No, this was a newfound level of contempt. A level that he was beginning to understand couldn't go without penalty.

"You're a walking excuse for an abortion, just because you beat the coat hanger doesn't me you can beat me. On the other hand, if you don't make any issues for me, maybe I'll let you keep working here for the rest of your pathetic life. But if you so much as breathe heavy, you won't be stocking chips anymore.

Instead, you'll be begging for them when you're living on the fucking street starving. Do we understand each other, sweetheart?" she asked, her tone drenching with sarcasm.

Stanley was so stunned by her harsh, despicable berating that he could say nothing. He merely stood there blankly, unable to comprehend how someone who was so beautiful on the surface could be so revolting beneath it. She reached out and wrapped her claw-like fingers around Stanley's jaw, her fake aqua nails piercing into his cheeks. She placed her other hand on his balls and squeezed while pulling downward, causing him to cry out.

"I know you're a little slow, Stanley, but you understand how to say yes and no, so let's hear it."

"Ye-yes. Yes," he cried.

"That's a good boy, I'm glad that we understand each other now." She loosened her grip on his nuts and pushed his face away disrespectfully.

After getting a talking to from Candy, he knew it wouldn't be long before she got in the old man's ear. After that kind of exchange, it was only a matter of time before Red was upset with him. His premonition held true. A few days after, Red gave him a menacing glare before instructing him to take a seat in his office.

He entered, already branded with an attitude of defeat, head hung low and tail between his legs. He was reverting back to the gloomy outlook that plagued his youth. A mental reset as he prepared for the worst like the Stanley of old.

"Stanley, please." Red gestured toward the chair.

Stanley did as he was told and sat. He rubbed his hands together, the jitters back in full swing as his leg rocked up and down uncontrollably.

"So, I know you're already aware of why I've asked you in."

Stanley shook his head solemnly, tensing to ready himself for an outburst.

"Just because you're a fucking idiot doesn't mean you can always play stupid, Stanley. You know damn well why you're here! Candy has made me aware of your issues in the workplace. She's told me everything you've been up to. How you've been staring at her, drooling inappropriately. How when your staring wasn't enough you moved on to trying to touch her." Red snarled through clenched teeth, trying to contain his anger.

"Now, Stanley, if you hadn't worked here for decades and weren't such a nitwit, I'd fire your ass on the spot. I finally find a woman I love, and who loves me unconditionally, and you dare to compromise that!? To disrespect me so openly in my own establishment!?" He was screaming rabidly now, suds accumulating in the right corner of his mouth.

Stanley sat trembling uncontrollably, fear paralyzing him from any kind of calculated action.

"You're lucky Candy should be so gracious, she's the one who saved you. She doesn't want you to lose your job and end up a filthy vagrant, even though that appears to be the mentality you harbor. No, you will continue to work, Stanley. But instead of getting the business next year, you will continue to run the routes and maintain your current duties. I've chosen to skip Florida and stay here with Candy. I'm still retiring, of course, but moving forward, Candy will oversee the affairs here. I'm afraid your actions are simply indefensible, and as a result, you're again back on the outside. Now get the fuck out of my sight."

Stanley still sat dumbfounded, shaking like a young boy missing his parents. He was deep out of his element, drowning in the shame of acts he never committed.

"I said get the fuck out! Now! Goddammit! Now!"

Stanley launched himself up to scurry out but before he could exit, Red hollered at him again, bringing his motion to a pause.

"Wait! I have a meeting with Utz this afternoon. Candy will be in the office when you bring back the deposit slip today. Give it to her but bear in mind, one more fuck-up, Stanley, one more incident of your imbecilic perversion and you're gone. Now you can get the fuck out."

He ran straight outside whimpering to seek refuge in his truck. He hopped inside and closed the cab, crying hysterically, snot bubbling from his nose, his salty tears pulled by gravity into his mouth. He glanced up through the windshield and back toward the building.

Candy stood outside the office looking back at him as she took a drag from the cigarette between her plump red lips and exhaled with a smile. She exuded a victorious flavor, blowing him a kiss as she finished her smoke and headed back inside.

At that moment, something inside of him changed, a conversion of sorts that threaded his psyche with indecencies, the likes of which he'd never dreamed he could fathom. The grimmest, most unspeakable visualizations stampeded across the sinister cyclone that was swirling inside him. He felt a strange kind of relief begin to take hold of him.

His tears stopped flowing. His snot dried up. He blew his nose into a napkin in the truck before starting the engine. A look of vengeance in his being, the disturbed man he'd always been was no longer docile. The beast had finally awoken.

He pulled up to Carpenter's Hardware and left the truck running. He stepped out holding a massive sack of coins collected earlier that afternoon. He moved inside the store, darting toward the outdoor tool area.

He settled on the chainsaw with a 20-inch blade. That would serve him most effectively, he'd decided during his earlier revelations. The brand was less relevant to him as it would only be a one-time use.

He dragged it up to the counter with authority, void of all thought aside from the certainty cemented in his expression. The cashier could see his streaky dried tears and derangement in full focus. He slammed the saw down onto the countertop, then lifted up the massive bag of change and smashed that down beside it.

When he pulled back up to the office, Red's car was gone as he had alluded to earlier. Stanley drove the car around the back of the building to the loading area and exited the truck. He grabbed the saw and two more massive sacks of coins and dragged them in behind him. When he entered, he set down his goods in an orderly arrangement.

He picked up a single sack of coins and made his way across the hall to Red's office. He stared down Red's door, his eyes tired and bulging, the image of mania impressed upon him. When he opened the door, he turned to see Candy sitting behind Red's desk, staring into a small pocket mirror while juggling between applying bronze facial powder and fluffing her hair.

"What is that?" she scoffed. "I'm not sure exactly how fucking stupid you are, but you're supposed to deposit those and bring me the slip, shit-for-brains."

Stanley paid her no mind, gently closing the door and locking it. She began to notice something was different, the push-over clay man was no longer willing to abide by the bitch's barking. No, instead, it was time for the dog to begin biting.

As he moved in closer toward her, the terror in her expression served as an indication that she understood the seriousness of what was happening. She cried out in horror, her attempts to evade him and hollow pleas would soon be cut short by the brutal violence that had been saturating his mind in the truck. He was ready to make his dreams come true. Stanley poised himself, eager to silence her, and slung the heavy sack of coins hastily upside her cranium.

The instant brain rattle left her seeing stars as she collapsed to the carpet. Her eyelids flickered as she reached for composure, but time dried up before that came to fruition. She was unable to sense the full sack now coming down with all of his momentum.

He drove it with a calculated excitement intended to be a deathblow. Her skull cracked, most of her previously perfect smile was now missing, and for a moment, she resembled a broken piano.

Her carefully sculpted nose was now pancaked— flattened in such a way that fixing it was far outside the abilities of the finest surgeon. He placed the next blows on her legs, listening to the violent crunch soothed him. Each snap and crack helped exhale a further measure of relief.

She was in a state of shock so deep that it rendered her incapable of speech or expression. She no longer had choices, her sole purpose now would simply be to absorb all of Stanley's frustrations, which were innumerable. With Candy completely immobilized and gasping on death's doorstep, he set the crimson-soaked coin sack down and trotted back to the loading area.

He stared down at the chainsaw as if it was the culmination of his life's work. As if everything he'd done in time was all designed to lead him to this precise moment. He wrapped his fingers around the handles and took a deep breath.

He sawed Candy down into about forty or so pieces, they were pretty compact. Apparently, he must have selected an upper-end model because it tore through a human like it was child's play. He tasted a new kind of comfort as her hot blood sprayed across his face, it all felt like it was meant to be.

Now, in her new form, Stanley could see the evil inside her. She was like a big puzzle, but no matter how you sifted through the carnage and put her back together, you got the same results. Ugly. It was ugliness that Candy hid so well from those she involved herself with, until she felt like lifting the veil. Now it was Stanley who had lifted the veil, permanently.

💰   💰   💰

Red walked up to his office door and opened it quickly, his tongue quivering with enthusiasm as he readied himself to plunge it into the mouth of his sweet Candy. But the visual in his mind was far from the one he would reveal.

Nothing could have prepared him for what came next. As the door swung open, the same loud, golden vending machine greeted him just like it always did. Except it wasn't stocked with the gamut of free snacks that normally stared back at him.

No, something much gristlier and more nefarious lay inside. It wasn't easy to tell what it was at first, the sloppy collection of body segments was ruthlessly force-fit inside the machine and unsurprisingly blood-drenched. Candy's hands and feet had been cut off, chunks of legs, arms, thighs, tits, and torso were also on full display. Her mutilated organs, torn from her chest lay propped inside and ready for purchase and pulverized.

The attractive head that Red had been fantasizing about smooching just minutes earlier was now in a condition so foul, it suffocated that possibility. It had been sawed off and placed on display in a way that it was staring right at him upon entry. If the concept wasn't clear enough, in fresh dripping blood, the words "TRY THE NEW CANDY" were running down the formerly transparent machine glass.

Red tried to yell but nothing came out. It probably wouldn't have mattered anyway because moments later, Stanley's large, bloody sack of coins blasted him from behind. Red fell down and struck his head on the corner of the marble coffee table. Stanley lifted his limp body up into the chair and duct-taped him securely. He then exited back out to his truck one final time.

When he returned, he had a large funnel in hand and a third, even bigger bag of coins. He sat down in Red's chair staring at him. An indescribable vileness festering as he waited for the old man to awaken.

About ten minutes later, he finally came to, confused and unable to remember the circumstances at first. Eventually, it all flooded back to him; the vending machine, the new candy, the hell. Stanley's deranged smile sat frozen on his face, beyond the reach of reason.

"Stanley, w-what are you doing?" Tears welled up in Red's eyes.

"You can keep the money," Stanley said through a twisted grin. He shoved the funnel deep down his throat while Red gagged and pleaded. He was now the one whimpering, he was now the dependent one and it was Stanley who held his life in his shaking hands.

He hoisted up the first large bag of coins and dumped it into the funnel, listening to the loose change roll down the plastic and into Red's esophagus. He squirmed and shook violently as the mix of copper, nickel, and silver weighed down inside him. The wanted to vomit but the funnel stretched his throat in a way where he just remained gagging.

Next, he reached for the second bag and began to unload that one as well. Red's gut was starting to protrude outward further and further, filling up with the heavy mountain of coins. His eyes widened to golf ball dimensions, popping a half-inch out as Stanley moved onto the third and final bag.

This one was the largest of the lot, containing such a mass of currency that Stanley needed to drop a few scoops in by hand before hoisting it up. The bag was still about half full of coins when Red's stomach ripped open. All of his guts and innards rushed out in a shooting wave of twinkling gore. His once pristine office no longer looked like a place of business. Instead, the business was all over the place.

💰   💰   💰

A short time after the murders, Stanley turned himself in, explaining his plight before divulging the monstrous details that he'd initiated. When it came to sentencing, he got life in prison without the possibility of parole for the savagery of the double-murder.

Everyone on the inside called him Psycho Stan after hearing the manner in which he killed Candy and Red, the twisted details didn't take long to circulate. No one fucked with Psycho Stan, his name alone instilled a healthy fear within the deviant populous.

Stanley found it odd that in prison people gave out the snacks at the commissary instead of using machines. He thought they were missing an opportunity to save a job by getting some machines in there, and if they'd have asked him, he would have had no problem restocking for them, free of charge. Their presence might bring back some fond old memories for him and if someone decided they wanted to fuck with him, who knows? Maybe they would end up becoming the next new candy.

Either way, Stanley had it made now. He wouldn't have to worry about having to run a business or work for the rest of his life. He had his three-square meals a day and zero bills to pay.

They even had a television in the prison. The inmates constantly bickered over which show to settle on. One thing was crystal clear though, every Monday night, even the worst scumbags in the joint knew that Psycho Stan would be watching his favorite wrestlers. Whether they wanted to or not, there wasn't a soul that dared to change the channel and interrupt while Madman Moses was on the tube.

He had people that now looked up to him, respected him, and most importantly, feared him. It wasn't quite the light at the end of the tunnel that he'd always had in his sights, but Stanley finally found the retirement he'd always desired.

THE DONOR

Just because you can't find the right guy doesn't mean you should have to go through life alone. Emily had tired of the unabated rounds of dating that never failed to conclude with her stinging disappointment. Society had reached a point where men had found a loophole, a clever way to cut out all the chivalry and romance. Now they were swiping in the morning, hooking up in the evening, and onto the next adventure before they digested the first one. Being stuck in an age of instant gratification created a complex challenge for Emily.

One that made any kind of non-virtual romance feel entirely improbable. Not being the most attractive girl meant it would take oversight of her oddly-shaped features for someone to understand the sweetness she offered. The shallow nature the culture fostered that she'd been forced to carousel through the last few decades made that seem even less feasible.

Her heart knew no boundaries, she was filled with wit and intellectual qualities but they did little to help her cause. Few would linger around long enough to comprehend Emily's—at first glance—camouflaged elegance. Her shyness always suppressed it initially. If only one of them would have the patience to hang around for long enough to break through it.

It had been years and years though. If a romance was destined to manifest, then the stars would have aligned long ago. Her body wasn't going to be capable forever. At thirty-six, she was pushing it already.

The now or never point of no return was already on the horizon. After much research and consideration, she'd decided the present, was seeming like the most logical path. She knew that with each day she waited, the lower her probability of conception plunged.

She couldn't have been more excited about her impending motherhood. Fertility clinics weren't exclusively for couples that were having trouble, it was also for the lesser glorified, would-be proud single parents too. Her contemplations were steeped with visuals of holding her newborn.

They triggered goosebumps; she could almost feel the baby nestled beside her. Finally, the house wouldn't be absent of conversation, a voice besides her own would be heard. She'd do all the right things and give the extra attention that partners couldn't. The full hundred percent, even the extra parts of which lovers usually allocate to each other. Her focus would only be on grooming the child with all the traits it would need to be successful and gushing an overflow of love, while providing a sturdy moral foundation.

They treated her so professionally at the clinic, coddling her into a supreme state of serenity. The process was quick and easy, she felt fortunate that everyone had been so caring toward her. Everything that happened that day only proved to reaffirm her decision.

The vindication was an intoxicating sensation. She'd finally taken the next step in her future. Soon, she'd be whole, but until then, she would rest and be careful to lead a more conscious, healthy lifestyle. After all, everything she ingested would now have a direct effect on her soon to be newborn, it would need to be only the finest moving forward.

After a few months, her belly had grown to a healthy rotund shape and her condition had now become obvious. She was fast approaching the magical day and, at the stage she was at, Emily considered her pregnancy sure enough to talk about. The last thing she wanted was to make an announcement to the few people she had in her life only to have a miscarriage. She told her mother and a couple of close friends about her decision and how far along she was.

They were more than ecstatic. They knew she'd been somewhat of a hermit over the years and always had a dilemma with men staying in the picture. Everyone understood but, of course, didn't utter the reality that this would be a wonderful milestone in an otherwise tepid existence. They all threw their full support behind her, knowing she may need some extra help since she was braving this on her own.

Emily's close circle knew the choice made was a heartwarming, calculated one. If anyone would give a child a love-infused upbringing while providing the sort of stability many of them only dreamed of experiencing growing up, it would be her.

The only queries they seemed to lodge were ones of a more curious nature. Artificial insemination was an intriguing topic not often broached casually, and therefore, when one came upon it, it would only be natural to have questions.

After the rounds of congratulations and reassurances had echoed for a while, they were all left with the same question: "Who's the donor?"

She could do little to quell their nosiness, in truth, she herself didn't know. It was policy to provide an anonymous experience on both ends as a means to avoid any potential unwanted or uncomfortable moments.

To her, it was of minor relevance, at least during that time anyway. She had no desire to know but realized her child at some point would voice a request to. Approaching that was more of a concern than revealing who was inside tube number twelve, but she would handle that situation when it presented itself. That was a conversation she'd have years to prepare for.

After some initial apprehension, she decided to tell them the little she did know. She'd requested a white donor with the rationale that if she selected someone that was her same race, the odds that the baby would resemble her would increase. She'd been told he was a craftsman with gray eyes and curly brown hair.

He was a religious man, although did not disclose his deviation, and his sign was Virgo. That was the cache of particulars she had about her baby's father. It seemed sort of silly to her that the donor's astrological sign was actually a field in popular demand. She snickered a bit each time she recapped the details for inquiring minds.

Emily had taken the time to think about him in her head, though sometimes not by choice. She'd had a reoccurring dream, a vague vision that included this blurred rendition of him. The dream lacked closure though, it seemed like it was more about her struggling to expose his mysterious appearance than creating a fictional interpretation of who she thought he was.

It just continued with her looking through this peculiar vision machine, kind of like you'd see at an eye exam. A blonde woman kept changing the lens but the appropriate prescription never seemed to drop in place. She couldn't grasp the inference, maybe subconsciously she wanted to know who he was?

Consciously, she knew she didn't—the demand had never arisen. She'd been too focused on the baby to waste time or thought on any of that. There were a thousand things she'd need to arrange and accommodate for; she didn't have time for herself, let alone imagination. She had someone else to think about now, she couldn't be selfish, even with her thoughts.

She'd just fixed herself an organically harvested salad topped with GMO-free grilled chicken when the phone rang. She carefully adjusted herself to get off the stool in an effort to make sure her protruding stomach didn't bump into the counter. The kid had been kicking a little bit earlier in the day and she suspected he might be resting now. It was best not to wake him.

Yes, she was aware now, the "it" title had transitioned into "him." She had cheated and checked the gender early, the anticipation had been eating at her. It was relieving in a way to know that even if she never had a husband, she would still have a man in her life. She grabbed her cell off the coffee table on the outskirts of the kitchen and answered.

"Hello?" Emily asked cheerfully.

"Hi, may I please speak with Emily Black?" A male voice inquired with a hint of suppressed tension shining through.

"This is she. May I ask who's calling?"

"It's Gavin, Gavin Marks from Plainfield Women's. Ms. Black, can I ask you to have a seat for a moment please?"

"Why, is something wrong? What's this about, Mr. Marks?"

"I have some news for you, just please let me know when you're seated."

Emily moseyed over to the love seat and slumped down in it, heart fluttering, almost afraid to tell him she was ready for the news. One thing felt certain, estimating from his tone, it couldn't be good.

"Mr. Marks, I don't mean to be out of line, but you're scaring me. Please just tell me what's going on?"

"I'm sorry, it's not my intent to frighten you but something's happened. Something that we have to make sure you're aware of. Now, normally, we don't divulge any information of this nature about the donor but we've been made aware of a situation."

"A situation, what kind of situation?" She tried to avoid losing her patience.

"Your donor, he's a man named Samuel Clovis. He appears to be dangerously unstable. The Westchester County police force were called to his house a short time ago. Inside, they found the mutilated bodies of his entire family. Everyone except him, that is. They believe… they believe he had something to do with it."

There was a lengthy silence. Emily was quite speechless although she had so many questions.

"Ms. Black, are you still there?"

"Yes, that… it's… that's so horrible but, but what does that have to do with me? He doesn't know who I am. Does he?!" she shrieked in terror.

"Our offices were ransacked and vandalized last night. Your files have… they've vanished. They might have been stolen."

"Oh, my God. You gave me the seed of a psychopath?!" She rose to her feet and began pacing.

"We do a thorough screening process, he had no prior history of mental illness. Zero. It's like he just snapped. They still don't know it was him for certain, this is all just precautionary really."

"His family is dead and he's missing, along with my confidential medical files I might add, and you call that precautionary?! Save me the sugarcoating, I know you wouldn't be telling me all this unless I was in grave, grave danger. He wants to kill me too…" Emily felt the true extent of the situation sinking in on her.

"Now, we don't know that. Don't worry, police are on the way to you right now, you'll be safe soon. I just called you so you'd know, in case you noticed anything strange."

Emily couldn't move now. Not only was she paralyzed with fear, but another presence had revealed itself. Her puzzling daydream was now understood and manifested as reality's disturbed equivalent. He stood tall and firm behind her with a rugged hand clamped tightly over her mouth, suppressing a now panicked breathing pattern. She felt a sharp, bulky metal blade pressed against her spine, cutting in carelessly as if there would be no threats, only a destiny that even a psychic couldn't have foreseen.

"Tell them everything's fine," he whispered to her, adjusting his grip.

She hesitated momentarily, pondering the repercussions of her limited options.

"I'm not going to fucking tell you again, bitch."

She had no idea what came over her next but something told her not to be quiet, she needed to tell Mr. Marks, even if it cost her. She had a feeling it would be costing her either way.

"He's here, help! It's hi—ughhgh."

He stuck the blade inside her with ease, grinding the unforgiving steel on her lower spine bone. Emily dropped to her knees in front of him, releasing the phone along with a horrified squeal. She wrapped her arms over her stomach in an attempt to shield their baby. The phone screen spiderwebbed upon landing before Samuel stomped it out for additional good measure with an animalistic belligerence.

"Daddy's home now, I bet you've been thinking a lot about me!" he said, waving the scarlet smeared knife around like an absolute fucking maniac.

His actions could only be described as unhinged. They had little to no relevance, a meaning even his own twisted mind couldn't gauge. He was headed somewhere savage, but the exact coordinates were largely unknown.

"Am I everything you hoped for?!" he screamed, stabbing at the loveseat repeatedly, ejecting long streams of white stuffing out of the couch with each motion.

"Please! Please! I'm sorry, whatever I did, I'm sorry," she cried.

"You wanted to let it continue. You wanted it to go on forever! Didn't you?! Didn't you?!"

She seemed baffled. Trying to grasp the denunciations of a madman can never be approached with much confidence.

"Let what? No. NO. I didn't. I swear I didn't! Please!"

"The master don't want us here anymore. We're needed elsewhere, there is a great war upon us and we've been called down. I received the messages yesterday, he told me to bring everyone... even the small ones... even you," Samuel said, flinging the knife into a piece of furniture.

He settled his mind on a last-minute substitution, venturing back toward the open door he'd crept in through. He raised a massive two-handed power drill and brought himself back around the kitchen table toward Emily again. The drill bit was the length of her forearm with enough girth to fill her eye-socket, although she prayed it wouldn't.

"But he doesn't even exist yet!" she pleaded.

"He does to me." He smiled while revving up the drill like a gear-head with his favorite muscle car.

The monolithic blade rotated, now associated with a sadistic determination that, in all probability, the tool's designer had never intended.

"He's not even grown, dammit! Please just let him grow, I'm begging you," she cried, her tone wet and messy with defeat.

"He can grow in hell!" he growled.

He plunged the weaponized sinister spiral into her belly, partially collapsing it. A river of red sprayed out like a loose fire hydrant would, except the color scheme was reversed, the red was on the inside, not out. Emily began to shake as the steel continued to jar her callously.

She felt their child kicking frantically inside her, aware something terribly unnatural was afoot and trying with everything to fend off the bedlam. It was the most atrocious of sensations. Suicide would have been more than welcomed, if only there were a way to evade the current happenings. The mixture of agony and horror squirmed in her belly with the gory drill bit.

What she witnessed next felt almost supernatural. Her prayers had been answered, painting the most beautiful horror before her that someone in her position could beg for. The torment needed to end by any means necessary.

Samuel's grip loosened on the drill as suddenly his upper skull was blown clean off the top of his head. His wet, exposed scalp splattered across the curtains before he slumped over sideways on the recliner.

He flailed his arms about like he was doing some sort of zombie seizure impression. Almost all of his head was missing. Emily had no idea people could still speak with their brains blown out, but somehow, the words blurted out.

"I'll be back… for… you…" he said while still making motions that appeared to be out of his control.

Emily plucked the knife from the couch cushion not too far from her and began to slam it through his cheek repeatedly. She continued to stab until his face felt like a distant memory. She'd only seen it for a few moments and now the recollection, as well as the physical representation, was destroyed. By the time the police reached her, she was just slicing up a pile of gore, sitting on top of her furniture.

She didn't convey any bother regarding her own body's blood-leaking condition, she was more focused on butchering the corpse before her. The authorities had to forcefully remove her from the property while she was still bound in her kill trance.

Still confined to her state of frenzy, the deranged screams she bellowed out about her baby showed that a switch had been flipped. A distortion in her mind that left a lingering corruption, she felt the fresh wounds of trauma as well as the mayhem from the material ones the donor had left on her.

That night, God must've been watching over Emily, the hospital was able to pull off what was the equivalent of a miracle. They saved her life, and in addition, they were able to save her child by delivering him early. There were some complications though…

♦   ♦   ♦

She decided to name the boy Edmon, which was a French name that stood for protector. He certainly was, the doctors told her that it was his face that had shielded her major artery from being shredded by the drill bit. If she wasn't pregnant at the time of the attack, she would have most likely bled out before she reached the hospital. Ironically though, she knew that if she wasn't pregnant, the attack would have never happened at all. What a strange paradox she was immersed in.

As a result of taking the drill damage for his mother, Edmon was left with a ghastly, deformed face. A face that frightened children and adults in unison, even the most tasteless souls hung their heads, shying from eye contact. The ridicule he was fortunate enough to dodge had nothing to do with compassion, just the pure surging terror that his presence spawned. A ghoulish, chewed-up mess that he awoke to each morning. The lone keepsake from his father—a man he'd never meet but could also never forget.

In a perverse, yet merciful irony, the event had left him an empty imbecile, unable to comprehend his own hideousness. Being born early more than likely was the origin of his brain damage, which was so severe that as he grew, he was unable to communicate with others. Just an empty vessel, wandering aimlessly, a walking argument for euthanasia if there ever was one.

The icing on this repugnant cake was how Edmon sounded. Not only did he look and act about as off-putting as possible, but the drill had also mangled his vocal cords as a final abhorrent bonus. His disturbed breathing was heard by his wheelchair-bound mother almost every minute of every day. Her ears serenaded by a sickening gagging noise that reverberated what sounded like shredded meat flapping in the wind each time he inhaled.

Emily thought about killing herself almost every day. Somehow, she raised him despite her crippled frame and decades spent pinned down by a suffocating depression which Edmon had no way of comprehending. Things that took her almost no effort previously she now had to work ten times as hard to achieve.

She'd been confined to a wheelchair beside her physically able-bodied son, cursed with the mind of an infant, too ruined to initiate the most novice banter. Waking up to stare down the cruelest of jokes every day as an immobilized shell of her former self.

He was now in his late twenties and she was still changing his adult diapers and cleaning the shit out of his asshole daily. Obviously, this was not what she'd envisioned for them. This looped, living nightmare would have broken any other woman ages ago but Emily dug deep and found a way to hang on, even if it was just by a thread. A thread of microscopic dimensions.

Nothing seemed to favor her anymore, there was no one left to help. Her parents had died years ago, her friends kept in touch loosely still but they couldn't come by often. This was primarily because Edmon's maturation resulted in significant temperament issues.

He was always even-keeled around his mom but if the dynamic changed, things quickly shifted to a more dangerous hue. Emily learned that her boy was hazard-wired with a hair trigger and just as soon as he began seeing red, others could be leaking it.

Each time they'd had company, he'd become remarkably violent—at first, just with himself. It started with him banging his skull against the concrete floor of the garage until he knocked himself senseless. It escalated to him gravitating toward knives and sharper objects before culminating with Edmon slicing areas of his body open and ripping out tiny handfuls of his insides. Emily still wasn't sure if these episodes were because of the guests or just part of the brain damage he'd acquired during birth.

This seemed to become clearer when a friend of Emily's, Belle, had planned on staying with her for a few months. The plan was to try and alleviate some of the stresses arising around her. The house had become overfilled with unnecessary items and trash. Belle aimed to help her clear out a few rooms in the house she just wasn't capable of attending to.

The thought was nice but the results weren't. The visit lasted all of three hours before Edmon grabbed Belle by the throat, beginning to sever her oxygen supply. Once he had her on the ground, he ripped a clump of her hair out and a carmine color began to infiltrate Belle's well-kept blonde hair.

He then removed some of the revolting feces from his diaper and put them into her mouth, while barking undecipherable grunts in his wheezy inhuman voice. Emily was thankful to have snapped him out of the episode finally, not daring to contemplate where it might have ended otherwise.

Belle was an angel and was the last standing pillar of Emily's support system. Unfortunately, that day, the final pillar crumbled. She'd always been her best friend and maybe that's what caused her to remain silent on the incident. She understood the hell and anguish she'd suffered for a few minutes was constant for Emily.

She explained after what happened that she could never come to the house again but promised to continue their relationship through phone calls and letters. That would have been welcomed, but regrettably, that would be the last time Belle and Emily communicated.

After the occurrences, Emily decided if anyone visited, not that they were lining up at this point, she would need to take some precautionary measures. It seemed she had no choice but to lock Edmon in his room to avert any other mood swings or disturbances.

She was relieved that she was able to procure the services of a nurse that came by once a day to help with a handful of chores and the medical issues she was still dealing with after the attack. But if the nurse was aware of the risk she was taking by being there, she most definitely would not be.

Although Emily had lost her faith in him, she still thanked God for the nurse. Ilene served her a sliver of sanity in an otherwise entirely demented routine. She enjoyed the casual conversation; it made her feel normal again even if it was only for about the length of a sitcom each day. It was something to look forward to outside of staring at and soaking in her wretched, hulking man-child's warped rituals.

She found a certain amount of her resentment over time had angled toward him, even though deep down she knew it wasn't his fault. She understood, that to some extent, this was probably a normal struggle that someone in her misery-knotted position would wrestle with. Her life was a bit lonely before, but if she knew this was the "man" she would be getting in her life as she was laying out her blueprint, she would have most definitely rethought the decision.

Without a second of hesitation and zero doubt, yes. She would easily give his life and her handicap to return to her prior state and arrangement. There were so many sinister thoughts dwelling in her mind since that fateful evening.

The fantasies she was inundated with were more than unhealthy. Thoughts of her killing Edmon, Edmon killing her, both of them committing suicide. They were always dangled on a thin string, an option for that rainy day or sunny morning. The weather didn't matter much to her anymore, everything felt gray.

Emily found herself more immersed in these thoughts, more so than her own reality. She was getting off to them in the way most people would from masturbation. She hadn't been with a man since she could remember, inserting her fingers inside herself while she recalled what was left of Edmon's father's face had become a nightly procedure.

Lightning would strike in her vision, transposing the slop pool of shattered bone and cartilage that was Samuel's face as she'd last saw it with their son's. The fantasy culminated with her eviscerating Edmon's face with the same knife she'd used on his father. She hadn't quite become the proud mother she'd envisioned.

Ilene had just finished cleaning up, she wished Emily a good night before locking the door on her way out. She'd left a small chocolate cake with a single white candle shoved inside it; a Bic lighter lay on its side in the vicinity.

That evening would mark Edmon's 27th birthday.

Regardless of everything that had happened, she couldn't overlook that. Of course, it was always still a taxing day for her, revising the mayhem in her head and playing out different scenarios and possibilities that could never actually transpire.

She'd decided she would prepare a little celebration for him, not that he'd understand what was going on anyway. She'd do it now while it was a bit later in the evening, keeping it closer to Edmon's bed time was a technique to avoid getting him riled up for too long.

She would let him out a bit now but remind him bed was soon before giving him his surprise and calling it a night. She snatched the Bic up and lit the lone candle before setting it back down. As she rolled herself toward his room and removed the keys from her pocket, out of the blue came a knock at the door.

At first, she thought she might be hearing things, until it happened again. She re-pocketed the keys and powered herself back, retracing her route until she reached the front door.

"Who is it?" Emily asked.

"It's Gavin, Ms. Black. Gavin Marks," the muffled voice explained.

"Gavin Marks? I'm sorry, I'm not interested, sir. I'm very tired—"

"From Plainfield Women's, Ms. Black. We helped you conceive some years ago."

"Plainfield Women's…" Emily stammered, feeling the shell-shock run through her.

"I just wanted to talk with you for a few minutes. Do you have just a short time to talk with me, please?"

She deliberated, really not sure why after all this time someone from the sperm bank would be reaching out to her. It seemed suspicious, but if it was someone who meant her harm, she welcomed it. She prayed that person was lying and she would open the door to find a gun pointed at her forehead.

She would tell them to stick it up their fucking ass and squeeze the trigger until the clip ran dry. She envisioned the bullets discharging from the barrel and tearing through her feeble frame. She quickly unlocked the door and gave the handle a newly excited tug, embracing whatever stood on the other side.

"Please come in, Mr. Marks, it's… it's been quite a while I suppose, hasn't it? The last time I spoke with you I was a young woman. Young and strong, a far cry from where I sit now, isn't it?" she chuckled, brandishing a playful yet pain-ridden smirk.

"Yeah, it all feels like ages ago. You look good, Emily," he said awkwardly.

The smile melted off Emily's face, she knew it was a ridiculous fib. She didn't need the pity; she didn't need the lies.

"I'm sure you didn't come here to recite wild exaggerations about my appearance, Mr. Marks. What actually brings you here, if you don't mind divulging?" She cut through the bullshit as politely as possible.

Mr. Marks seemed to be growing upset and highly emotional all of a sudden. He tried to compose himself before speaking but was having a hell of a struggle.

"I've… I've lied to you, Emily."

"It's alright, you were trying to be nice, I just haven't been well," she confessed. "I haven't been well in a while now."

"No, that's not what I mean. I lied to you a long time ago. I lied to you about your donor." Tears now overcoming him.

"What do you mean?" she said, flabbergasted.

"This is so hard." He paused, regaining his composure.

"The sperm they gave you that day you conceived; it didn't belong to Sam Clovis."

"What do you mean? I don't understand, if it wasn't his then why would he have come for me, for us, that day?"

"I put his name down on the form but it was wrong, I forged it."

There was a red-hot silence that felt paralyzing.

"But I still don't understand, why? If it wasn't his… then whose was it?"

Mr. Marks continued to quietly sob while mustering all his courage.

"It was mine," he cried.

A look of confusion, followed by rage, followed by devastation paraded across her face. She was a soup of feeling—boiling to a scalding rate. Emily now also found herself weeping, staring at the fading, liquifying candle on Edmon's birthday cake. Thinking back to that horrible afternoon, 27 years ago to the day.

"I had a problem, sexual issues. I was a sick person, women never seemed to find me attractive. So, this was my way. My sickness evolved with each day I was ignored. You understand, right? Just like you, this was my only way to have a child."

Emily had no words for him, she could only stare blankly and listen as his tear-drenched babble.

"But I got help, Emily. I'm not that person anymore. I never could find the nerve to tell you. I'm a fucking coward. Every year though, every year I thought about it, I even parked outside your house a few times. I should have helped you; I shouldn't have let you bear this burden alone. If I hadn't switched the names, things would have... he would have never come here. Everything that happened, it's all because of me! I can't, I just can't do it anymore! I can't live with myself, with what I've done. I want to make amends. I'll do anything, I need to make amends." Mr. Marks stared down blankly at the flickering fading flame on the lonely cake.

Emily rolled over to the nearly dissolved birthday candle and blew it out.

"If you had any idea what I've been through, any idea what we've been through. If you had a clue, you'd understand that's impossible, Mr. Marks. You can't pick up a thousand fucking pieces! Do you understand me, goddammit! You monster!"

"I'm so sorry, I know I can never make up for what happened. I know you will never forgive me. I can accept all that. All I ask is, please, just give me a chance. I just need a chance to help, please."

Emily's attitude changed, a calm came over her in a clean wave as she cleared her mind. Not quite letting go of the rage but maybe focusing it.

"You know, back before your son was born, I'd always assumed one day he'd ask about his father and I wouldn't know how to address it. Now he can't because the man who I was told was his father robbed him of that ability. Robbed him of that and both of us of so much more. I thought he'd never get to meet his father. Do you really want to do something for me, Mr. Marks?" Emily inquired devilishly.

"Yes, Emily," he whispered, still sobbing.

"All I'd ask is that you wish your son a happy birthday. Do you think you'd be able to do that?"

Mr. Marks nodded his head while continuing to weep. She picked up the sad-looking cake covered in the dried wax that had bled all over and handed it to him. She pushed herself toward Edmon's room, guiding Mr. Marks to his fate. Once she reached the door, she again removed the keys from her pocket and looked him in the eyes.

"Are you ready to meet your creation?" she asked, exuding delight for the first time since God knows when.

Mr. Marks nodded again, trying to prepare himself for something there was no way to prepare for.

She opened the door to a dimly lit room, the floors covered in garbage and filth. A smell permeated that could turn a stomach inside out in a matter of seconds. Mr. Marks stepped inside accepting of the unknown, accepting of any outcome in an attempt to close the gap on the spiritual disparity that haunted him. The uneven karma that had come to put the hooks of guilt into him, the domino effect that he was solely responsible for.

Edmon was not fully visible, he sat in a chair that was set in the corner of the room staring at the wall. His frightening breathing could be heard faintly but he remained unresponsive. The darkness that clouded him left so much to the imagination. Thoughts began to edge into the back of Mr. Marks's mind. He was beginning to reconsider his decision just as Emily slammed the door behind him and locked it.

She waited outside and listened to the screams. They didn't last long, maybe the length of a radio tune and, in that respect, the bloodcurdling cries were, in her twisted universe, music to her ears. She was almost sad when they ended. It was over now; it was all over.

HOUSE SITTING WITH DAD

It was just after my thirteenth birthday when my dad told me we had to house sit for his friend, Joyce. House sitting seemed more like a chore, not something you would try and get your teenage son geeked up about. Dad was really good at dressing stuff up though; he could make a trip to an inner-city playground sound like a vacation to Disneyland.

Around our relatives, friends, or anyone he thought was better than him, that's exactly what he did. He bragged so convincingly that he often was able to erase memories from my own mind of the many times he'd disappointed me before. He was like a magician, except he didn't own a suit and reeked of Budweiser and cheap cologne.

He was never really great at planning things, but he did teach me a whole bunch. I had the joy of knowing and seeing things that the other kids my age didn't. He let me watch really violent movies where the people died in bad ways and sometimes the ladies in them took their clothes off too.

He always told me about how I should never hurt anyone though, what we were watching was just entertainment and that if I ever did and someone found out, they would lock me away. If I was locked away then I couldn't have sex with the ladies when they took their clothes off.

Sometimes we would watch other movies where the ladies were just having sex with the guys the whole time. They usually wouldn't stop until white stuff came out of the guy's penis and went all over the girl. Dad would usually explain exactly what they were doing, often answering my questions before I asked them.

Other times, they would use weird objects on the tapes too. They looked like something out of my toy chest but shaped really funny. One time, there was this movie where two ladies were playing around together.

The blond-haired lady was having a tough time pulling marbles that were stuck on a rope out of the other girl's asshole. Dad knew exactly what it was though, he could be really smart about certain things. He told me that was only for the girls though and that no son of his was going to be a faggot.

I began to really enjoy the tapes, so much so that I had spied on Dad to see where he would keep them. That way, I could watch them more when I was by myself. Something about watching them with him was starting to feel strange, I felt like I was getting much too excited now to watch them together anymore.

I wondered if everyone had tapes like that or just Dad. At first, the thought of going to someone else's place with Dad to housesit for the night seemed boring but I became interested when I started wondering if maybe Joyce had other tapes like Dad's. Maybe some new ones that would excite me even more. I'd watched my father's almost a thousand times now, it never got boring but something new would be nice.

Joyce was already gone by the time we arrived. Dad fished the key out of her mailbox and stuck it in the hole. When he opened the door, we stepped into Joyce's kitchen. She sure had a lot of roosters inside; they were on the walls and the table and the dishtowels. I'd never seen so many before.

Dad immediately ripped into the 30-pack of Budweiser that he'd brought with him. He pulled three through the cardboard and placed the rest of them in the refrigerator. He suggested that we check out the house together next, see what the place was like.

I guess Dad had never been inside. He only saw Joyce at his house or the place people go to drink. It seemed massive from the outside but once we started to take a looked around inside, it felt a little tighter. Dad told me about how Joyce lived alone and didn't have too many friends. That probably explained why the house was so nice and clean with all the extra time she had on her hands.

As we entered the living room, I'll never forget what we saw next, mostly because I've never seen anything like it since. For a woman who lived alone, she certainly had a lot of seating. A giant blue sofa stretched around the living room but that wasn't the strange part.

Across the whole back of the lengthy sofa was an arrangement of porcelain dolls. Mostly of similar sizes, but visually, each one was unique. Every hair color, eye shade, and outfit you could think of, all mixed and matched with the pasty skin that only these creepy dolls were known for.

It didn't stop there. We went through the whole house and with each new room there were more and more of the creepy dolls. Dad clarified it for me a little further, revealing that Joyce was a "real weird bitch that needed to get laid." He explained to me how he'd tried "fucking her" before but believed "she was playing for the other team" since she was able to resist him.

When we got to her bedroom, Dad told me that's where he'd be sleeping and I could have the couch. I wanted to tell him that all the dolls down there freaked me out but there were almost just as many in the bedroom so it wouldn't matter where I slept, there would be no escaping them.

The doll closest to me had the most menacing smirk of the lot, stretching ear to ear. Her dead eyes staring through my soul, her long, curly red hair highlighted as it laid over her white dress.

This doll seemed like it was positioned in the focal point of the room and was a bit bigger than the others. I couldn't help but continue to stare at it when, suddenly, it lunged forward at me, jumping off the dresser. I was stricken with fear momentarily until my attention was drawn to a husky black cat that had been seated behind the doll.

My father laughed at me as I gazed into the feline's green reflective eyes as it sat still atop the dresser defiantly and unflinching. Once Dad settled down, he told me the cat's name was "Kit-Kat" and validated his prior theory about Joyce, saying, "I told you she liked pussy." The cat jumped down and scurried out of sight and Dad put the doll back in its place.

After that, we went back to the living room and watched a movie called "The Sicko." It was about a man that would stalk women for long periods, kill their mothers, and then study their grieving process. The man liked to make obscene phone calls to them also.

Dad really liked this movie a lot. He seemed to really enjoy the parts where the girls cried and contemplated suicide after losing their moms. For some reason, the girls in the movie liked to have sex a lot after their moms died. Dad really liked that about them too but not quite as much as when they cried.

He didn't make it to the end of the movie, most

likely because he'd drank about 25 beers or so already. Dad could sure put them away. At times, I questioned how he could even physically keep it all inside him. Add the beers to the "medicine" he would have me help him take most days and you'd probably be more surprised if he was awake.

He taught me how to help him take it a few years ago. This medicine started out in a powder form but he would have me heat it up in a spoon to liquify it as part of the prep. Then Dad told me to suck up all the liquid with a syringe and press down on the plunger a bit until it "pissed out" a little, to get all the air out.

He said if any air was left inside, it could kill him if it got into his bloodstream, so I had to be extra careful. Then he had me tie-off his arm to get his veins bulging and noticeable before inserting the needle into him.

I'd got really good at finding Dad's veins since the first try when I'd needled him about a dozen times or so. He struck me in the face each time I fucked up, so that really helped motivate me to learn it quicker. One time, he hit me so hard that one of my molars cracked in half. I spit it into the trash with a bunch of blood and now each time when I get ready to find his vein, I stick my tongue in the hole to help me concentrate a little better.

After so much hands-on training and Dad's stern inspiration, I could usually do it on the first try. I really liked the beginning of the injection, pulling some of his blood into the tube and mixing it with the medicine before pushing the whole load inside him.

Dad got real relaxed when the medicine hit him, so much so that he usually passed out for hours and sometimes his eyes would roll into the back of his head while drool leaked out of his mouth. He never did tell me how he got sick or what the medicine did for him.

After I pulled the syringe out of his arm, I wiped the blood off with a napkin before setting it on the coffee table. I knew now with Dad out for the count I could look for Joyce's videotapes without restriction. Most of the obvious places I looked didn't turn up anything significant. There was still an overwhelming excitement of the unknown inside me, I was looking forward to something different.

I continued the search but I didn't find anything. Still, I was not letting that get me down. I had all night, if something was there, I'd most definitely find it. Finally, I made my way back into her bedroom and began to rummage through her dresser drawers.

She had a collection of the objects the girls liked to stick inside each other from Dad's tapes. I fiddled with those for a few minutes before checking under her mattress and under her bed. Finding nothing else of substance, I headed for the closet.

I opened the closet door to a spacious walk-in that was closer to the size of a spare room, filled with about four times the amount of clothes one person would require. Again, there did not seem to be anything noteworthy except for one set of items. Inside a beautiful wooden chest, I'd noticed there was a fake bottom.

After removing the entire contents of it, I popped up the barely noticeable purple velvet finger hole to discover a full-sized doll costume. This included a dress, shoes, wig, and even a porcelain mask. Dad was definitely right; Joyce was a real weird bitch.

I'm not sure why, but next I grabbed hold of the doll mask and slid it on, a feeling inside was pressing me to try it on. After I did, I decided I would continue wearing it throughout my scavenger hunt.

Those creepy fucking dolls throughout the house wouldn't mess with one of their own. I couldn't help but feel as though they were watching each move I made, this would provide me some protection on my journey.

With my new safeguard, I placed the trunk's contents back inside exactly as I'd found it and turned out all the lights in the bedroom. Thankfully, before leaving I realized I'd left the closet door open, which would have been a dead giveaway to my snooping. When I turned around, I saw something that I hadn't before since I was looking into the closet now with the light off. An eerie, faint orangey light illuminated from the ground inside, almost calling to me.

I approached it with plenty of reservation, understanding this was an unnatural thing to be glowing inside a closet like that. I walked up to the wall feeling around on it when, suddenly, one of the panels sunk in slightly, followed by an unlocking sound. I slowly pushed open the hinged barrier and proceeded forward into a tiny radiant hallway.

I didn't have to duck my head but I felt like any adult venturing inside probably would. I walked further down the tunnel, which was lit from above and padded all around with a soft kind of charcoal toned Styrofoam material. After a few more steps, the passage took a sharp left and I trudged up another ten yards or so before approaching a second door.

It was making more sense now why the house seemed much bigger from the outside, there were hidden areas within it. The door was covered with more of the grayish Styrofoam but had a single peephole dead center. My pulse was pounding with excitement, Joyce probably had a lot of tapes if she was hiding them so secretly. Maybe she had enough to where I could smuggle one out unnoticed, that would be unreal.

I stepped up and peered through the hole, curiosity getting the better of me before I could decide if I should. Through the distorted fish eye lens, I viewed something I was not prepared for. Something so alarming that, in essence, confirmed Joyce was not a normal woman. If building a secret tunnel in the heart of her home wasn't hair-raising enough, the chamber of horrors inside brought things to a whole new level of abnormal.

Inside, I could see a girl standing limply, whiplashing her head against the wall repeatedly. Her forehead was raw and shredded, I stood in awe watching the blood drag its way across her face. Globs of her removed flesh had been hammered into the wall, apparently by her own dented skull.

She was naked all but for a filthy, blood-spattered t-shirt that only hung down to about her ribs. Her arms were clearly restricted somehow, she appeared to be shackled to the wall. Unlike the women I'd seen in Dad's tapes, this woman's pussy was overgrown and hairy. Dad said that hairy was the best way for a woman to be, he let me touch his stubbly face after he shaved and asked me, "Now, would you want to put your carrot on that?"

Again, just as when I had seen the light coming from the closet, I didn't hesitate to venture forward, regardless of how scary the situation seemed. Somehow, I was calm and at peace, I felt like I was supposed to be there. When I entered the room, the girl did not acknowledge me and just continued banging her head aggressively. I'm not sure why but I enjoyed hearing the constant thuds.

There was a different kind of smell inside. It reminded me of the time I'd found the rotten raccoon behind our school in third grade. Just like back then, it triggered my penis to solidify, making it even harder than the times I watched Dad's tapes. I found that strange since it was purely triggered off a scent, whereas all of my other boners had been caused from the movies.

I looked to my left, an angle that was a blind spot when I'd first glanced through the peephole and noticed another girl dressed like a life-size version of the dolls around the house. She was propped up at a two-seat table and seated in an unnatural way. The attempt seemed to make her appear as though she was sitting at a table but the results, for many reasons, could not convey that.

To start with, she had been destroyed without mercy, that much was obvious. Her eyes had been removed completely, a generous ring of crusted blood was slathered around the sockets while the deeper insides were pulled outward like two pits that were puking.

I also noticed this girl's mouth was agape and her tongue had been severed. The girl also had three-inch spikes that had been beaten deep into her earholes. The wounds were all infected with a foul, inky rot displaying the most advanced stages of decomposition. She was a complete mess, robbed of many of her God-given senses.

I began to think this might be why the other woman was still yet to acknowledge me. She just continued to thrash her skull against the crimson wall, creating a constant pulsating spatter. As her head flailed about, I could recognize the living woman had gone through a very similar treatment. Many of the same signs applied to her but, somehow, she was still alive.

I yelled at the woman a few times asking her what was wrong but she still couldn't give me a response. That's when I started getting the ideas. All the murderous films and disturbing things that Dad and I liked to watch together I now had a once in a lifetime opportunity to try. Like Dad said, if anyone found out, I'd be done for but in this house, the people were already dead and destroyed.

I could help Joyce out a little really with no negative aftermath and explore the feelings that I might never get to otherwise. If the police or anyone found out about Joyce's secret spot, she would be to blame, seeing as she'd started the killing long ago.

If she came home to a new dead girl, what was she going to do, tell my dad? No, she'd just have to deal with it and find herself a new one. The mangled lady would probably kill herself if I didn't anyway, why waste a chance to get my feet wet?

I knew I needed to calm her down first if I was going to get this done. Maybe if I gave her some of Dad's medicine it might get her to relax a little. I returned back and Dad was still out cold, he appeared to be breathing but now it smelled different near him. When I reached into his pocket to get more medicine, I could see that his pants looked quite wet and a darker fluid had soiled them. He smelled like freshly pooped diarrhea. I took a closer look at him to make sure he wasn't waking up. I knew he noticed that I had taken any of his medicine that he would be really upset with me. I was relived that he stayed silent.

When I returned back and approached the distracted bizarre girl, she was still occupied by her self-destructive activities. I'd found a selection of tools that were just out of the reach from the girl which might assist me with stunning her long enough to stick Dad's needle in her. I'd chosen a small ball-peen hammer, it wasn't too heavy for me and I know if I struck in the right places it should bring her right down.

I decided to retreat briefly and do a practice run on the dead doll woman a few times before going at the living one. I was aiming for the joints, mostly focused on collapsing the kneecap in the wrong direction. After a few strikes, I began to lose myself. I became more aroused with each strike, the mayhem strengthening my already thickened penis.

Before long, it wasn't a practice session, my pants were down and I was on top of the table ramming my throbbing member into the black rot within her eye socket. With each thrust, a chunky wave of dark decomposition fluid blew out and when that socket was drained, I moved onto the next one. By the time I was finished, my thighs and belly were covered in a browning red gore.

I had done it, I was no longer a virgin but I didn't feel too different. I patted myself on the back mentally for removing everything I was wearing (except for the doll mask) before starting, otherwise, I would have had a much harder time concealing my deeds.

As excited as I was, still nothing had come out of me like I saw happen to the men in the movies. Maybe I needed someone who was alive still to help me along. Either way, I was growing tired of contemplating if that might be the case, it was time to see for myself.

It took me about three swings to get her knee to fold the opposite direction, just the way I'd envisioned it. She made no effort to fight me, instead, she only crumpled to the floor. I followed up with another strike and landed a direct blow on her right temple.

Her body seemed to be involuntarily jerking when I tied off her arm. It made it hard to aim the point, I stuck my tongue in my cracked molar and focused. Just like Dad taught me. I already had the syringe loaded up and as soon as her vein popped, I dumped the medicine into her bloodstream.

I also had a big serrated knife near me that I'd brought along with the hammer to experiment with while I was inside her. Maybe being inside her in more than one way could help me get where I needed to. It was really difficult at first to get her to relax. She was dry and unlike the dead girl's eye-sockets, I was having a tough time moving in and out of her.

I jammed the big knife inside her hole and the jagged blade tore her all to hell. All the blood made it so much easier to get a rhythm going. Her seizures were already causing her to gyrate so I was unsure if she had any reaction to me putting the knife in her. Either way, I was feeling heavenly, smelling the decay from the dead doll paired with the living girl's convulsions was so lovely.

As her eyes spun up into her skull, a chunky vomit blew out of her mouth and made me quiver. I continued pounding on her. I was going so hard that she must have lost control of her bowels; liquefied shit began to spray from her anus all over my testicles and thighs. She was beginning to remind me of Dad and I think that's what drove me to pick up the knife.

I stabbed her so much that I needed to take breaks

in between. I stabbed her so much that the knife blade snapped at the mid-point. I stabbed her so much that I could see her heart after I collapsed her chest.

I continued sex with her while I watched the life drain out of her eyes—not that there was a whole bunch to begin with. I put my hands into her opened chest, touching them both to her heart and felt it fluttering into my fingertips.

I found an unbroken rib on each side of her torso and wrapped my hands around them firmly. Then I paused to regain my wind before what I hoped was the finale. I started pushing myself inside her with as much force as I could possibly muster, using her ribs as leverage to pull her into me with each pump.

Her heart was now literally jumping out of her chest and looked as if it might explode. I just needed to keep going a little bit longer and I should've been able to finish her off. She was almost there when both of her ribs snapped simultaneously, leaving two bones sticking outward like tiny animal antlers.

It looked like she was trying to scream but she had no tongue so it didn't sound like much. I don't know why I was upset, maybe because her ribs had broken on me or maybe because I wished she was Dad. While still inside her, I picked up the hammer and went to work on her exposed heart, smashing it to a bloody pulp. She finally stopped moving.

Somehow, I still hadn't made it to the place where the guys in Dad's tape had. Nothing came out of me, maybe I wasn't doing it right. Regardless, I'd had more than enough fun for a lifetime, no need to get hung up on one small detail and spoil the evening. After I was finished, I had to pee really bad so I just did it inside the girl before removing myself.

I headed back to Joyce's master bedroom to take a quick shower before retrieving my clothes in hopes to avoid staining them. I had wiped any dripping fluids off me with the table cloth to avoid trailing any outside of the hidden area but I was anything but clean. I entered the bathroom still wearing the doll mask and closed the door behind me.

When I turned around, I noticed that Kit-Kat was sitting on the toilet in front of me, motionless, again unwavering and confident. I wasn't quite sure what to do next when Kit-Kat leaned in toward me and started to lick.

It seemed that maybe the kitty had tasted these kinds of fluids before. He must have really liked them since before I knew it, all of the blood, piss, shit, and decomposition fluid had been licked clean off my pecker and body.

I then opened the door and he left me while relinquishing a satisfied purr. I probably could have just gotten dressed with the kind of cleansing Kit-Kat had performed on me but part of me still wanted to take a shower. I showered wearing the doll mask, cleaning it and drying us both off once I finished.

After that, I went back into the chamber and got dressed. I wanted to place the girl I'd just killed at the table with the dead one I'd molested but thought better of it, not wanting to dirty myself again. Instead, I grabbed Dad's medicine needle before putting the mask back into Joyce's chest and leaving everything as I found it. The sun was almost up now, I could see a flamingo-colored sky peeking in behind the window blinds.

I stayed up watching Dad the rest of the morning while Kit-Kat sat on my lap until he finally woke up.

Luckily, he was sitting on a big blanket when he shit himself, so we were able to bag that up with his shorts and underwear and throw it out at Slater Park.

Dad was the kind of guy who could be found shaving at sunrise inside a Hooters bathroom. Passing out or sleeping in his LeBaron was a common occurrence, so thankfully, he had a spare pair of shorts in the trunk.

A couple years later, Dad was diagnosed with HIV, which looking back on it, I may have given him inadvertently. I wondered if he may have gotten it from the needle I put in the woman I'd murdered.

I would have thought for sure if anyone would have been exposed to it, surely it was me. I played around inside the woman for hours. I was completely covered in her by evening end. Maybe I was exposed to it, but regardless, the thought didn't make me feel any different.

Dad shot himself in the head a few months after his diagnosis. I found his body one afternoon when I returned from skateboarding. He was naked in the tub without any water, it was hard to translate the final expression on his face since the majority of it was missing.

Much of the left side of his skull and brain had been plastered against the mint-colored bathroom tile. The blood and mint kind of reminded me of Christmas, which often causes him to cross my mind during the winter holidays. His suicide note talked about him not wanting to go on with people thinking he got "the fag's disease." In his note, he made no mention of me.

I'll always wonder what became of Joyce and her doll collection—the literal one and the figurative one. I will always look back on the night Dad and me house sat for her fondly, it was by far my favorite memory with Dad.

It was probably because he was knocked out cold the whole night and, of course, because of the secret hallway and doll room. That night changed me for a lot of reasons, it planted a bottomless motivation within me more than anything.

Someday, I'll work really hard to graduate from high school and set my sights on college. Then I'll be sure to work even harder in college. Forget about the girls, the parties, and friends, I'll just be working. Then once I graduate from college, I'll put all the other stuff in my life on pause and strictly focus on my career.

Then finally, once I hit that milestone and find a job where I can make lots of money, I'll have enough to pay for a big house of my own. I already know exactly what I want. I want something big. Something roomy. Something deep.

A place I can call home and maybe make a few changes too, so it suits me perfectly. I have some very specific areas in my head that I'm thinking of. I won't stop working until I get it. Ever since that night with Dad, I always knew at some point, I was going to have my very own dollhouse.

FIVE O'CLOCK

SHADOW

Jim Gitty had been in business since the 60s. He owned a small two-seat shop that had been passed down from his father. It was a quaint clean place where men could be men without a filter. In the event that lightning struck and a lady popped in with a kid or something, they were able to put on a nice gentlemanly facade until they were once again amongst their own. Although, he couldn't recall the last time that had even happened.

2019 sounded like a number Jim would only have heard on the Jetsons, but somehow, he was there. The music had changed, the clothes had changed, the technology, people's attitudes... everything had changed. But not Jim Gitty, his shop was still the same.

Same vintage red, white, and blue colors twisting in the barber pole hanging outside. Same poster on the wall offering hairstyles from when Nixon was still in office. The classic smell of Clubman emanating throughout the place added a noble touch that should have been a throwback, but at Jim Gitty's, that was current.

His pop had handed the shop down to him and he never felt the urge or need to update. He still had dark, forest green pump chairs sitting on the black and white marble floor. The sky blue wall tile ran halfway up before turning into scissor patterned wallpaper. A picture of his father still hung on the wall in the back as if he was still watching over the shop. Everything just felt so perfect the way it was.

To him, it was all about keeping that good feeling alive and well, continuing the memories that made the place more than just a spot to grab a trim or a shave. Jim didn't cut hair for the money anymore, he'd paid off the building long ago, which included his living quarters upstairs. It was all he needed; it was all he wanted.

He reasoned it was a good thing he didn't need to cut hair to pay the bills anymore, his client base was shrinking by the day. Each time he opened up the paper, it seemed like another one of his friends was on the inside. But they weren't the talk of the town, they were just advertising for their final goodbyes. That was the sad part about getting older, watching your friends die and all the goddamn funerals.

The decor in the joint didn't help attract any new prospects or younger folks either. None of that mattered though, Jim was just keeping the shop open mainly to see his pals. He had a handful of regulars that liked to come in for a shave and a chat, maybe exchange a dirty joke or two in the process.

When the clients weren't sitting down, Jim was. He had a leather armchair toward the back, with an old tube television he liked to watch westerns on during his downtime. When he got tired of those, he might sweep up the hair around the chairs or sharpen his scissors.

Walter was by far his humble establishment's most frequent guest. He hung around so much that Jim joked about charging him rent. He also took the liberty of branding him with what he felt to be an appropriate nickname. One day during his typical appearance, he jested, "It's like you're the 5 o'clock shadow in here, can never get rid of you."

His reasoning being that he was usually posted up in the shop every few days right around five, just like clockwork. This obviously was a wily barber pun, which Jim loved to execute if the setup was right… and there was no better setup than Walter. He was a constant walking punchline, but at the same time, could spew them back with ease.

Walter was usually either looking to BS for a while or grab a quick shave and trim, his ritual bordered on excessive. He had a pretty dense but well-kept beard, he liked having Jim clean-up the parameter and prided himself in keeping a balanced, pristine look. Even though these were elderly men, they still committed to looking sharp. Jim always made good on their pact.

The conversation was always fun and, at times, eventful. They'd start with the most current news and work back to the good old days when things just seemed a whole lot simpler. Walter was good like that; he was a good shit and he typically came in with a joke or two. Last week's exchange was particularly amusing, even more than usual.

"What has 100 balls and likes to screw old ladies?" Walter asked excitedly, not wanting to wait for a reply.

"Oh, Jesus, what's that, Walter?"

"Bingo," Walter replied.

It was about ten to five when the bell on the door gave a hesitant jingle. Jim had just finished changing the blade out of the straight razor and set it down before turning his attention to the entrance. Walter stepped over the threshold slowly, more calculated than how he normally barged in, acting like he owned the place. He was dressed nicely in a beautiful dark blue suit and pants. He had on a pair of black leather shoes so glossy that you couldn't help but stare at the glare they gave off.

Still, he looked a bit off, like he was maybe a little under the weather. Jim had just lined him up on Tuesday so he couldn't be there for anything outside of shootin' the shit. He had to give the old bastard credit, he was pushing through just to appease him (or maybe himself) with some banter. He didn't expect anything less than that from him but didn't want to toot his horn too much either. "Nice suit, big shot, but you're not looking so hot, kid," Jim ribbed.

"That's funny coming from you, when's the last time you didn't wear jogging pants? If I wanted any shit out of you, I'd squeeze your head," Walter fired back.

"You know, if you were sick today, I wouldn't have minded a day without your mouth."

"I'm not sick, I need a trim and a shave, Jimmy."

"What do you mean? I just cleaned you up on Tuesday, it's Friday, there's nothing there, goddammit, what you want me to take the skin off too?"

"I want you to take the beard off."

Jim's eyes widened in astonishment, the disbelief overwhelming him as adrenaline pumped into his already racing heart.

"Walter, you've had this thing since I've known you. In fact, I don't think I've ever seen you without it."

"Yeah, well, I suppose it's about time then, isn't it?" Walter said, plopping down in the chair a bit slouched still.

Jim walked over, grabbing the barber gown and draping it over him, still befuddled as he readied him and tied off his neck.

"What is that smell? Didn't get a chance to hit the shower today, kid?" He half-joked, trying to stomach Walter's funk.

"Is this how you treat all your customers? It's because of smart ass comments like that, that this place has more open appointments than Dr. Kevorkian."

"I'll overlook the out of character scent if you tell me why you're all dolled up and wanna lose the beard all of a sudden," he asked, drilling further, his inquisitiveness peaking.

"I have an event is all."

"An event? What are you running for office for Christ sake?!"

"I'm seeing my kids today, okay!? You know I hardly see 'em, I don't wanna show up looking like some riffraff, alright? Listen, I told you, when it happened, I wanted you to do it. Why is not important, I'm a man of my word."

"I just… I never thought I'd see the day."

"Well, it's here, Jimmy, just deal with it already."

"Alright, alright."

Walter paused and locked eyes with him through the mirror, the kind of look that stares right into you.

"I just want you to know that I appreciate you having an old rat like me around here for so long. My kids being out of state and all, these days that we spend together, they're really all I got, my friend," Walter confessed, offering a rare glimpse at his emotions.

"You kidding? You're doing me a favor, at least you have kids, all I have is this place and Pop over there." Jim said, gesturing back to the wall behind him bearing the framed photo of his father.

Walter smiled back at him, watching as he picked up the clippers from his station and brushed them off scrupulously.

"Time to pick your poison, how do you want it, kid?" Jim asked.

"Take it all off, bring it right down to the skin."

"Clean shave?"

Walter paused for a minute as if considering it, then he looked at him again before removing his glasses.

"Nah, leave it at five o'clock," he decided, now grinning ear to ear.

Jim returned the smile, a part of him had always wanted the inside joke they'd shared for ages to come to life and Walter was giving it the green light.

"You're a funny guy, you know that?" he replied.

"I'm serious," he said, handing over his glasses.

Jim didn't wait for him to rethink it. He popped the number 1 head on the clippers and started going to town. Slowly, he pushed off huge clumps of curly gray hair from his face and watched it drop down to the floor.

He hadn't seen that much hair around the chair since God knows when. It was such a beautiful well-maintained pile he was accumulating, the thought crossed Jim's mind that this might be the last time he saw something like this again.

The warm spring day had brought in a few flies that were buzzing about the shop. They kept circling him while he was cutting the beard before landing on Walter. Jim paused to grab the traditional, vintage yellow swatter off the wall. He brushed a fly off him, causing it to stir upward and smacked it across the room. For a man of his maturity, this one-shot accuracy was pretty impressive.

"Still got it," he bragged.

He continued to shave off the beard, buzzing it down just as requested. He was a few clips away from completion when more of those damn flies started hovering around him again.

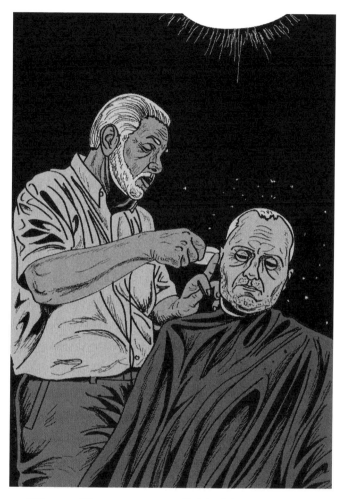

"Damn flies, can you tell it's May yet? Friggin' things are everywhere," he complained.

"Jimmy, I don't give a shit if they land on me, I gotta get going soon."

"Alright, alright, relax, you're almost done now."

He took a few more minutes to work the scissors and snip a little more off the top. Even though he didn't really need it, Walter said he wanted the works and he didn't feel like catching any more shit from him. Some short ticks later and Jim was done.

He stepped away from Walter to reveal a unique sight, new to the universe. He was shaved all but for a youthful five o'clock shadow that remained on his face. It was tightly aligned, despite Jim rushing to accommodate his requests. He'd needed to leverage the decades of carefully accumulated expertise to give his good friend one of the best damn haircuts he ever had is his life.

"You look like you're on your way to grab a six-pack and head to the drive-in. I can't believe it! You look like a kid again, Walt!"

"Thanks, but I'm already spoken for," Walter said while pointing to the wedding ring given to him by his late wife.

Jim brushed Walter off and applied the aftershave to his surrounding, clean-cut areas. He then flipped the barber gown up extravagantly as if he were unveiling a personal masterpiece. Walter rose up from the chair and stood proud, he had the look of a new man about him. He reached into his inside pocket and retrieved some folded currency. He looked at the small cluster of bills before handing it over to Jim.

"No, you know I don't do this for money anymore. Honestly, seeing this much hair around the chair is payment enough. I might just leave it here a couple of days, make this place look like a real barber shop again," Jim said, refusing the offer.

"How do you expect to stay in business when you're giving the place away?" he asked.

"You know me, Walt, I'll find a way. Just go have some fun with your kids."

Walter kept his eyes on him for another moment before shaking his hand and heading for the door. The bell started to jingle again as he pushed it forward but before leaving, he looked back once more.

"Jimmy, don't forget, you were always my guy," Walter said before completely exiting.

Jim turned on the old tube television a few minutes later before taking a seat in the recliner. The iconic opening scene in Once Upon a Time in The West played in the background quietly while Jim extended his arm to the small side table and grabbed the newspaper.

He hadn't had a chance to read it yet, the front page was still a little moist from the morning rainfall that had seeped into it. Thankfully, the humidity in the shop had dried it out enough to make it readable.

He decided he would head to the section he dreaded most. If he could get the obituaries out of the way first, then he could enjoy some of the less morbid current affairs. He flipped a few pages in and aligned his eyes to the top of the section.

So far, he was in the clear. It looked like there wasn't anyone he knew, thank God. Some poor teenager he'd read about dying in a horrendous car wreck topped the list. Then a few older nice-looking ladies, followed by a well-known priest. He didn't have a personal relationship with him but knew others that did.

As he continued further down the page, he froze, blinking several times believing what he was viewing couldn't be possible. The obituary read:

"Walter J. Mancini, 69, passed away Wednesday, May 18, 2019. He was the beloved partner of Paula Mancini for 43 years until her passing. He was born and raised in Central Falls and survived by his daughter, Melissa Allen, of Westfield Connecticut and his son, Daniel Mancini, of Framingham Massachusetts. He served during the Vietnam War before taking a job at the Osram Sylvania, where he worked until his retirement in 2004. He will be greatly missed by his friends and family; his funeral will be held at the Morten Funeral Home on May 20th at 6:30 PM."

Above the writing sat a youthful picture of Walter, with the same smile Jim had watched come through his door just a few minutes ago. It all defied logic, was this some kind of misprint? Was he going crazy? There were only so many possibilities, yet somehow, the supernatural explanations seemed just as likely as the more grounded ones.

There was no way to know with any certainty, but he was damn sure going to find out. Jim quickly locked up the shop as fast as he could and headed for the funeral parlor.

That trip wouldn't provide many more answers for Jim. If anything, it just created more questions. He overheard Walter's kids making remarks about how "weird dad looked without his beard" and more about how "inconvenient" the drive was. Jim knew that his buddy Walt deserved better than to be remembered as an inconvenience—a pain in the ass, sure, but inconvenience was a mischaracterization.

The whole time Jim sat there in his jogging pants and t-shirt listening to a priest make comments that really had nothing to do with Walt's life.

The people might have been dressed nicely and presented themselves well but as the thing went on, it was clear that he was the only one that really knew who Walt was. The only one that understood his humor and knew what was under the rugged callus that his violent, often unmentioned, years in the service had left upon him. Not to mention his years with the wife…

When Jim got back to the shop, he sat down in the chair, closed his eyes, and said a short prayer for his friend. In his heart, he knew that somehow that day, Walt's real funeral happened in his shop.

His kids were so nonchalant about his death that they waited to until the day of his funeral to run his obituary. It's like he knew Jim would have missed it, so he somehow found a way to pay him one last visit. One last visit that would leave him with a final punchline that would last a lifetime.

Jim opened his eyes as they began to tear up, still looking down at the floor where, a short time ago, he'd given his friend his last haircut. Now somehow all the hair that he'd so proudly left right in plain sight had vanished. The five o'clock shadow was no more.

STILL UNDER
CONSTRUCTION

They had been in New Orleans for about two days, both of which were mostly a blur. Travis and Wendy chose an odd place to commemorate their undying love for each other and play out their honeymoon, but not odd to those that knew them best.

They were drawn together like magnets, mainly because they were equally infatuated with the macabre and absent of the squeamishness naturally ingrained in most of their peers. They sought out the experiences that made people wince and fidget with discomfort. To them, seeing the horrors that average people were never intended to in their mundane lives was their calling.

They'd already stayed at the Lizzie Borden Bed and Breakfast, visited the Vent Haven Museum, and Villisca Axe Murder house, amongst dozens and dozens of other sites that piqued their ghoulish curiosity. Finding fucked up places that displayed bizarre objects or landmarks where disgusting things had happened was something they'd preoccupied themselves with almost entirely during their pre-proposal dating window.

They had just married a day prior almost completely by themselves, save for their "priest" and a drunken vagrant they'd persuaded to serve as their witness. They'd slathered each other in a fiendish corpse-paint and used a grim encirclement of death as the scenery for their wedding. They stood with eyes locked and hands clenched tightly in one of New Orleans' oldest graveyards; the St. Louis Cemetery.

It originally opened in 1789, quickly accumulating a variety of crypts and unsettling gothic tombstones. It was built outside of the city limits, mostly due to the fear of disease, as people in those times believed it could be transmitted from the dead to the living. There couldn't have been a more appropriate backdrop to cement their bond than the mass of aged, above-ground burial chambers encased in sharp fencing. It was everything they dreamed of and so much more.

A sinister yet fulfilled feeling hovered within them as they kissed overzealously, smearing the greasepaint around their lips and chins. They continued their passion for a few more moments in front of the justice of the peace (who looked much closer to the devil than a man of the lord) before slowly exiting the towering gates.

Their fingers interlocked as they moved at the pace of zombies. They plodded onward with expressions and attire that made them look more like they were leaving a funeral than concluding a wedding.

Wendy was garbed in an all-black dress with matching nail polish, lipstick, and high heels. Travis had a midnight tux that covered him entirely except his neck and hand tattoos that still crept into visibility. His hair was gelled backward into a clean fade and his eyes were masked with a dark, non-reflective pair of aviators. Something about their apparel choices made them look like brother and sister, not that it mattered to them anyway.

Their post-marriage celebration kicked off with bottomless glasses of alcohol that rotated each round until they'd tasted almost every poison known to man. Climbing to that rung of inebriation, of course, makes you want to dance next, so dance they did, everywhere from where it was encouraged to the line at the taco stand. They were in a party city so that wasn't too out of the ordinary.

What they did to culminate the evening certainly was though. Travis had a lightbulb go off at about 4 AM and they headed back to the Saint Louis Cemetery to seal their vows on a random gravesite. Old "Archibald Randle" wouldn't mind they were sure, it would probably have been the most action he'd seen in a thousand years.

They awoke sluggishly in the graveyard the following morning, the stench of sweat and spilled alcohol clinging onto them. They tried to remember how it all went down to no avail as the hot sun began to cut into their dreams.

After a night of intense, morbidly romantic debauchery and sleeping most of the day, it was time to continue on with their nocturnal excursion. The honeymoon was over and it was now time for them to scratch another item off the bucket list.

Yes, they came to New Orleans to get married, they wanted to validate their bond in one of the wickedest, most magical and bizarre places an American could venture to, but they also chose to get married there because of The Museum of Death. Obviously, the history of the location and atmosphere was phenomenal too, but if they were being completely honest, they'd come there primarily to see the Museum.

They'd heard so many horror stories about people becoming ill, running out screaming, fainting... you name it. It was supposed to be one of the most evil, disturbing attractions that the west had to offer. A place for anyone but the faint of heart. Somewhere they'd been clawing to get entry to for what felt like an eternity and now, finally, they were mere moments away from admission. It was time to see if everyone was a less extreme version of their own personas, or if the hype was legit.

As they drew closer to the old decrepit storefront, the familiar imagery from their research sunk in, up close and personal. An enthusiasm came over them, the glow from the sharp orange letters that spelled out the establishment's name floodlit across their faces through the weathered glass windows. A pair of paintings showcasing a skeleton woman as well as a finely-dressed skeleton man tipping his hat displayed in the main windows. To the left of the artwork, written in bloody lettering on the glass, it read:

"The MOD may cause violent headaches, seizures, epilepsy, PTSD, appetite loss, double vision, divorce, and many other problems."

"Divorce already, huh?" Wendy said, elbowing Travis and snickering at the notion.

A bit further below that, after a melting Satan face, it continued on:

"ENTER AT YOUR OWN RISK, ABANDON ALL HOPE YE WHO ENTER HERE!"

They looked at each other and exchanged a rushed kiss before hurrying through the doors. When they entered, they were greeted by a creepy-looking fella; about what you'd expect from a place of that nature. His clothing seemed quite dated, it was hard to tell if that was intentional or not. He wore a dusty top hat, purple vest with a white-collar shirt extending outward and a black cape specked with flakes of dandruff. He palmed a cane that was capped with a decomposing head, and as they neared closer, he tilted forward peering over the purple lenses of his glasses.

"Good evening and welcome to the Museum of Death. I'm the host of the grounds, Drexel. From what I gather, my typical spiel needn't be repeated for either of you. I sense that you know exactly why you are here," he said with a mischievous leer.

"Oh yeah, we've been waiting a long time for this," Travis said, confirming his intuition.

"Of course, you have," he replied confidently.

"We'll take two please," Wendy chirped.

Drexel reached down for the ticket which bore the museum name in a circle around a skeleton head. He grabbed his hole-puncher and clamped down on the tickets through the right eye of the skull's face.

"When you've done this job as long as I have, people like the two of you are easy to spot. If you want to review the list of warnings and legalities for your amusement, they are on the back of your ticket. Otherwise, enter at your own risk. I truly hope this experience stays with you," Drexel said in his best sinister voice.

They both thanked him and entered a bit more cautiously than they did the first door. It might have been Drexel's creepy insinuations or possibly some of the warnings that gave them the willies for a heartbeat or two.

Most likely, they were just the bait to make people feel as though the experience was so intense that they simply had to see it just for the sake of the story alone. Being able to say you survived the Museum of Death was a badge of honor. In the queer, exclusive target group of freaks they fell into, it was the badge everyone strived to wear.

The first room was filled with animals, which for Travis and Wendy was probably more difficult than most people. There was something about slaughtered animals that made them sad, even more so than if they were to see humans.

They associated a helpless innocence and frailty with them, but it was more the house pets that bothered them than anything though. The ones that society had groomed us to treasure. Needless to say, when they entered the room and met face to face with a taxidermized German Shepard's head on a stick, they didn't take time to look at the alligator bones, or anything else for that matter.

After the short-lived exploration of the first room, they made their way into the next, which was much more palatable and aligned with their style. The maroon walls of the second space were filled with what, by today's standards, was deemed "Murderabilia." A collection of real-life items, letters, documents, and artwork from the most depraved killers throughout history.

There was everything you could imagine, from John Wayne Gacy clown paintings to handwritten letters from BTK, to an old jacket that Ted Bundy had supposedly worn when he cut up a college co-ed. They were fascinated by this room and spent about fifteen minutes or so before wondering what was next.

They soon found out when they entered the adjacent area which was tighter but appropriately painted black, seeing as it was dedicated to Dr. Death; Jack Kevorkian. It was littered with his murky but compelling saturnine paintings.

Once you looked at one, it was hard to take your eyes off of it, they brimmed with an evil uniqueness. Travis and Wendy would have given anything to hang one on the wall at home. They seemed to both gravitate toward an eerie one of a man on his back being sucked into an enormous skull.

They also had two replica devices that they inspected, the first being the "Thanatron" which connected an IV line to the patient and routed into three separate canisters. When the patient pressed the button, the canisters would release saline, barbiturates, and finally, a fatal mixture of potassium chloride, which would typically shut the heart down right away.

The second device was the "Mercitron" which was essentially a gas mask fed with a carbon monoxide canister. While Dr. Death certainly intrigued them, he didn't tap into that same gruesome fascination that the dastardly humans who chose to take life without asking first did.

After surviving Kevorkian's quarters, their excitement was elevated by the next room. The high-profile murder room more than satisfied that perverse hunger they salivated over. The walls were littered with blown-up pictures of the most graphic, appalling class. You had everything from close-ups of Nicole Brown-Simpson's near decapitation, to Sharon Tate's torn pregnant figure.

This was a fun examination for them because they'd had some concept of everything they were looking at, but the museum did a great job of offering some of the lesser-known details of these highly mainstream crimes. They spent close to a half-hour reciting their own details about the various crimes to each other before moving on.

The purple walls in the following room tied in nicely to the Heaven's Gate theme. Apparently, the museum had made its own recreation of the mass suicide by the well-known cult. Some of their presentations included the actual beds that members were found in after taking their deadly potions.

The mannequins looked very eerie, clad in the same black and white garb and Nike sneakers, draped with the iconic purple sheets over their upper bodies. Just walking in there, you'd be hard-pressed to spot any variance between the actual crime scene and recreation.

There were many other exhibits available to view, including one that displayed the real severed head of French serial killer, Henri Landru. After that discovery, they continued to peruse the grounds before making their way to the rear of the building. As Drexel indicated, nothing was too much for them to handle so far. The end consisted of a small theater that offered long, soft velvet benches for their patrons to park themselves on.

Just as they entered the room, multiple people were exiting. Not the kind of exiting where things have just wrapped up and you're casually ready to finally head out, but the kind of exiting where you're running. Running from something you fear. The ambiance seemed to indicate that whatever was in the back was strenuous to endure.

One woman hustled, hand over mouth, as if trying to keep her food down. It didn't quite work; as she lost her brief battle with her bodily intuition, she discharged a nasty gagging noise and deep belch. Her watery vomit burst through her fingers as well as above and down below them, spraying indiscriminately and nearly tagging Travis in the process.

She was heaving violently all over the floor now, when suddenly, out of the shadows, Drexel appeared.

He aimed his outstretched arm at a black sign that showed a stick figure man like you'd see on a restroom door, puking everywhere. The sick stickman was overlapped by a red circle with a line through it. Beneath the international prohibition sign, it specified further: No Barfing Allowed.

"Can't you fucking read!? We make it quite clear upon entry but still every day somehow it happens!"

He handed her a barf bag and grabbed her by the arm, "If you can't handle it, don't watch it! Let's go! Move!" he yelled before dragging her off.

They were somewhat shocked by his rude behavior, but at the same time they understood, when you're scrubbing vomit off the floor every morning it can probably get a little irritating. They stepped over the woman's puddle of purge and walked toward the back of the dimly lit theater.

They both turned around simultaneously to take their seats, revealing what the woman and others who'd scurried away were watching. A solemn seriousness overcame them, Wendy closed her eyes before forcing herself to return her gaze back up.

"Oh, my God," Wendy moaned.

"I know, this is beyond sick," Travis concurred.

Thus far, aside from the initial murdered animal display they'd been caught off guard by but still powered through, nothing had come close to striking a nerve. Their thick-skin was penetrated as they looked up at the theater screen; it brought them to a different place. They were now face to face with what looked like the mangled and nude corpse of a dead 12-year-old girl.

She was laid on a metallic morgue table, a heaping portion of her face missing, her rigid tongue protruding out of the gigantic hole in her head. A monstrous man whose face was obstructed by a surgeon's mask leaned over her with shears. He expended a tremendous force as he clipped through the tiny specimen's chest cavity, snapping through the bones and cartilage while he grunted.

This vile footage continued for over ten minutes without intermission. It's like they were intentionally beating the audience down with it, making it feel never-ending for the sake of developing some cerebral scar tissue on each visitor.

About halfway through, another couple entered the theater and peered over at them. As soon as they saw what was on the screen, they turned around and headed right out. The woman looked back to them, shooting a dirty, judgmental glare.

"You believe that one? She made it through every room in this fuckin' place and now she wants to act like Mother Teresa," Travis said with disgust.

"Hypocrisy at its finest," Wendy piled on.

Once the long exercise had finally completed, it was clear there was no way they'd be forgetting any second of the child's dissection. The sadistic imagery that they'd witnessed was now burned into their minds, branded until they reached that very same table and the cycle repeated. Wendy pulled the ticket back out of her pocket and flipped it over. It indicated the following:

"Our feature today, 'Happy to Live, Born to Die,' runs on a non-stop loop in the back theater. The film is approximately one hour."

Wendy looked up at Travis, not wanting to be the one to say it, but she did, "You think we'll make it through a full hour of this?" she asked, pointing at the stub.

Just as she made the statement, a horrific film of a man on a motor-cycle crashing into a wall and turning into a human hamburger was shown. The video then switched to a brief clip of what looked like a man's torso that had a lion's head fused to it.

Travis attempted to answer the question but before he could, two men were jumping off a bridge with their hands interlocked as the camera followed them until they hit the concrete. Their bodies came apart, erupting their wet glistening flesh out and upward. The film was now moving at a much faster pace than the introductory scene they'd walked in on.

"This is pretty rough, I mean, I've seen similar stuff on the internet and Faces of Death, but this is really intense. It's part of the show though, we have to, right?" he said, looking for her to cosign.

"Yeah, of course, dude. We have to," she confirmed.

Wendy's eyes darted around the room trying not to focus on the film anymore. She needed to think of a method to get her out of there without looking like a chump to her new husband. Her next pitch wasn't the entire solution but at least it was a start.

"Hey, I really have to pee though, I'll be back in a couple, tell me what I miss. Okay?"

Travis looked at her, well aware of what she was up to but decided not to razz her too much. "Okay, hurry back though," he said as creepily as he could.

Wendy scurried off through the theater curtain, relieved to get away from the relentless death. She'd seen similar videos before too, but not ad nauseum. Also, the age of the girl and animals being jumbled in created a greater mental hurdle than anything from her past. She made her way down the long hallway that the restroom sign had directed her to just thankful to get some air.

When she reached the end, she noticed a set of stairs tucked away opposite the restrooms. She took a few cautious steps down until her eyes landed on another display simply titled "Mr. Doctor's Oddities." Maybe it could be her out from the movie, she could attract Travis to something potentially eviler than what he was currently entrenched in.

She moved in a little closer and peered down noticing the door at the bottom of the steps had a rectangular sign across it that read, "Still Under Construction." Now her antenna had raised and she felt like being nosy, but before she was able to pry any further, Drexel, seemingly out of nowhere, appeared again.

"Now you were the last one I thought might have a problem with reading, my dear," he confessed.

"No, I'm sorry, I didn't see the sign at first. What's down there anyway?"

"Everything and nothing all together, it's magnificence, but unfinished magnificence I'm afraid."

"Mr. Drexel, please forgive my forward request… but my husband, Travis, and I, we were just married last night. Your museum, this atmosphere, it's why we chose New Orleans, the Museum of Death was our destination. I would gladly pay you triple the entry fee if we could just quickly see the exhibit. Even if it's not done yet, it would create the most unique, memorable experience for our honeymoon. It only happens once you know," she pleaded with him.

"Mrs.…"

"Junkin. Today and moving forward, it's Junkin."

"Ah, I see. Congratulations, Mrs. Junkin, however, you're speaking with a man fresh off his third marriage and furthermore, I saw you in there," he said pointing down the hallway back toward the theater. "I see everything here, the dread on your face was all too obvious. If you can't endure what's in there, how do you expect to withstand what's down there?" he concluded, pointing toward the downstairs room.

"Whatever it is, I can handle it."

"And how, pray tell, do you know that, Mrs. Junkin?"

"Because… I've been through some really traumatic experiences outside of this museum of recollections." Drexel's expression still didn't seem convinced, triggering her to reveal further detail, "I'm a rape survivor." The revelation created an awkward silence that she let Drexel marinate in a few more moments before continuing. "I'm not trying to be so personal, but you asked," she defended, looking down toward her feet sheepishly.

"I was violated by three men and beaten within an inch of my life. You see this scar on my neck?" she asked, pointing to a white discolored slash mark. "This is where he cut me. A little deeper and I could've ended up another story within these walls. So, if I can handle that, then let me ask you a question. Do you think I can handle what's through that door?" she asked rhetorically.

"Fine, as you wish. But listen, like you said, the cost is triple."

Immediately, she pulled out four more twenties and stuck them into his palm tactfully, "Thank you, thank you so much, you've really provided us with a memory that will last for eternity."

Drexel pocketed the money and looked toward her once more, "Don't thank me just yet, Mrs. Junkin," he replied, a maniacal laugh leaving him that she assumed was intended to freak her out. "Meet me back here with your husband in five minutes."

Wendy nodded at Drexel before heading back down the hall and through the theater curtains. Travis's face was wrinkled with pain and anguish as she retook her seat beside him. She made sure to angle her gaze toward her husband instead of the screen. She tried to talk over the screams the film continued ejecting toward them, "Travis, I have a surprise for you."

"A surprise?"

"Yes, but you have to come with me right now."

At first, Travis still thought she might just be trying to get out of the movie, but as she explained further, a giant smile crossed his face. He knew they were about to see something unique, something that other people hadn't seen. They wondered what it could be.

The anticipation was killing them as they walked back down the hall. Wendy whispered to him, explaining the extravagant lie she'd used to convince Drexel to allow them entry. Travis seemed rather amused at the violent but convincing fib.

"So, you pointed to your neck gash you got in the jet ski collision? And he bought it?" he asked in disbelief but still proud of his new wife.

"We're about to go in, aren't we?"

"Dude, you are a true genius. Mr. Doctor's Oddities huh, what kind of weird shit could be in there?"

"Rest assured all your questions will be answered when you step inside, and then you'll have so many new ones…" Drexel surprised the couple by appearing with a response, followed by a cackle. Travis and Wendy laughed along with him before Drexel straightened up and cleared his throat. "Ok, a few housekeeping items before you begin. After I open this door, I have to lock it. I cannot have anyone else wandering into this attraction outside of our arrangement."

"Wait, what? How are we supposed to get out if you lock it?" Travis's newfound nervousness was evident.

"The exhibit is a straight shot through, once you reach the end, there's an unalarmed emergency door you must use, it only opens from the inside and will lock automatically upon your exit."

"That doesn't seem safe, what if there's a fire or something?" Wendy asked.

"Great question, and that, Mrs. Junkin, is precisely why this exhibit before you is still under construction… because it's not ready. There is, of course, a certain risk associated with anything. Now, will the building burst into flames when you step over the threshold and the door locks? Maybe. Anything can happen. But it is you who requested to see the unfinished exhibit, so it is you who must weigh that option."

They sat in silence entrenched in deep thought and contemplation, a new nervousness circulating through the air.

"If either of you are afraid, I will happily give you the additional payment back and thank you for wasting my time," Drexel sneered.

"Open the door," Travis commanded, apparently not caring for his courage to be questioned.

Wendy looked at him with less conviction, but she had made her bed and now it was time to sleep in it.

Drexel opened the heavy metal door and pulled it backward, he flipped the light switch on the wall, activating a dim flickering glow that outlined the path below them. He signaled them forward with his hand as if magically allowing them entry.

"Good luck," he said, releasing his coarse cackle once again.

They both stepped inside and listened to the door slam closed behind them, the sound was synchronized with the instantaneous injection of dread and regret bubbling in their guts.

"I really don't like this," Wendy whispered.

Travis stepped closer to her and gave her a kiss in the middle of the faintly lit corridor. He was frightened too but also thrilled. "It'll be fine, this is gonna be a story that we tell people forever, babe. Don't worry, let's just go check this thing out."

He let go of her waist and started moving onward. "Thanks again for doing this for me, you're really sweet, you know how much I love fucked-up shit like this."

"Don't thank me just yet," she responded, echoing Drexel's prior remarks.

They walked close together following the only route the basement offered. After a few more minutes of walking, they came upon a set of empty glass exhibition cases.

"This better not be it. If that weirdo hustled us, I'll go right back up there and kick his ass," Travis threatened.

"I'm sure there's something further up, this is probably just the part that's still under construction, remember?" she said, trying to calm him.

"True."

He picked up his pace slightly, and a short time later, was approaching a new set of exhibit cases, these ones were not empty. They were filled with something that looked a little familiar, something that didn't look real, it couldn't be real. At least they hoped it wasn't.

In the first case was a man's torso with a lion's head where a human one should normally be. There were no legs or arms and the body was impaled on a stake that ran up through its anus. Equally concerning, across from it sat the female example with both breasts cut off.

Again, mounted with an inhuman head that looked to have belonged to a horse but it was difficult to tell. The decay was more advanced on the woman— maggots swarmed the whole piece and dead flies littered the floor of the case. The female genitalia had also been replaced with that of the male horse's, leaving her quite well endowed.

"This can't be real, right?" Wendy continued to mumble, not quite knowing who she was being quiet for.

"I don't know, it's fucking twisted as shit though. Were you looking at the screen upstairs when you came back to get me? I feel like I remember this lion head," Travis vaguely recalled pointing back toward the first exhibit.

"Yeah, let's keep moving though, this place is fucking disgusting," she replied, beginning to move forward without him.

It didn't take them but another minute or so to reach the next exhibit. Once they did, they immediately wished they hadn't. What they came upon contained an adult corpse that was balled up in the fetal position, with a leg extending upward that was severed at the hip.

From the hip sprouted a variety of arms that were infused into the leg with a thick stitching and extended in all different directions. Again, the bugs had made their way into this display case but they weren't the only thing crawling around inside.

Three malnourished babies frolicked about, seeming joyful enough. One climbed up the remains and used the arms like a child might, swinging back and forth on a tree branch. The other pair sat feeding on the pile, pushing their raw gums into the rotten flesh and swallowing bite-sized wilted portions. The few tiny teeth that stemmed out were bloody and broken, they didn't seem upset though, as if the display case was all they knew.

They noticed as they approached them the babies had no reaction, they just continued to gum down into the putrid tree and rummage through the body parts and insects. Upon further inspection, Wendy noticed the reason they hadn't reacted to them was because their eyes had been sewn shut. The culmination of everything she'd taken in caused her to regurgitate it back in the form of a high-pitched shriek, followed by other hysterics.

"Travis! What the fuck is that!?" she yelled, listening to her voice echo throughout the corridor.

The babies all stopped and turned toward them immediately. They initiated an inhuman cry that something so undeveloped shouldn't be incapable of. Water began to bleed out, forcing itself through their wounded eyes as they rubbed them feverishly, harder and harder until the clear turned crimson.

"I don't know but you gotta keep it down!" he said firmly.

Abruptly, the already faint lighting cut out altogether and the babies stopped crying. The couple hugged each other in the lonely darkness, listening only to Wendy's trembling breathing pattern.

"What do we do, Travis? I don't wanna die, please don't let me die," she begged, shaking uncontrollably.

"You're not gonna die, we're gonna get out of here now."

Before he could finish his sentence, Wendy's whimpers were joined by a hissing sound that could be heard emanating from all around them. The smell in the room changed to something unnatural. They tried to communicate but a haziness pushed its way into their brains, stunting any thoughts before they could flourish. They both passed out in each other's arms hitting the floor with a hard thud.

When Wendy awoke, it was still pitch black—either that or she'd gone blind. She was terrified to learn that while she could speak, she could not move or feel her body from the neck down. The panic had spiked, her brain was still having trouble comprehending what was happening.

"Travis! Travis! Say something, dammit!" After a few more attempts of yelling into the darkness, she was finally able to conjure a response.

"Wennnnnnddddy," Travis projected sluggishly.

"I can't, I can't move, babe. Can you move? Tell me you can move!"

In the midst of her pleading screams, the lights suddenly came back on. She wasn't blind at least, although a small part of her started to wish she was.

Wendy would no longer need Travis to answer her question, it was all right there before her eyes, right across the hallway.

Wendy arrived at the realization that she was not only looking into a glass but also through one. She sat frozen, gawking through her own encasement while also peering into the glass cube across from her that housed her husband. They'd somehow been confined in the cores of the two previously empty displays that they'd passed in transit during their initial exploration of the hallway.

She took in a sight that by any account would be difficult. Her newlywed husband's head had been stapled onto the body of a dog. It was a young pup, resembling a Sheepdog. The canine's physique struggled to hold up Travis's head, it had already fallen over a couple of times when trying to gain its footing.

Travis's tongue sprung out from his mouth, drool now draining at a rapid speed. With his new hairy figure, he continued to try and stand on all fours but the weight of his head just couldn't be supported on such a disproportionate frame. He pushed his paws up, elevating the head about halfway when the staples burst and it ripped clean off. The head fell under the animal's stomach, facial expressions jumbled like a machine malfunctioning.

Travis's head tremors resembled the dog's, its body jerked, losing control of the most basic functions. A richer, blood-charged urine rushed from the Sheepdog and rained down on Travis's dying mind.

Wendy let out a bloodcurdling moan that would have awoken the whole graveyard. Drexel again stepped out from the darkness, interrupting her trepidation. This time, he was with someone else.

A large oafish man who looked eerily familiar, the surgeon's mask obstructing his face just as it had in the movie. It was the same man that had been shown in the theater cutting open the young girl on the table. His latex gloves were matted with blood and hair and he held a duffel bag at his waist side that appeared to be moving.

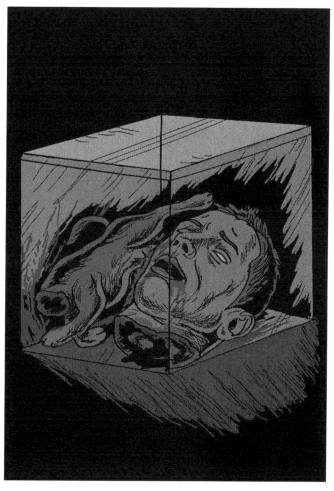

"You didn't put enough staples in him, look at this! Unacceptable!" Drexel said, scolding him.

Wendy quieted down having no idea what she should do now, her options were almost non-existent as it was. The duffel bag again began to stir about in an even more agitated manner. They turned their attention from Travis's decapitated, pissy head over towards Wendy. The closer they got, the more the bag shook.

"What have you... what have you done to us!?" Wendy wailed helplessly.

"Now this, Mr. Doctor, I must say is by far some of your best work," Drexel praised, pointing toward Wendy. "It looks like we just might be missing one thing," he continued eyeing the duffel bag.

Mr. Doctor lifted the flailing sack up and reached inside.

A considerable amount of time had elapsed since Travis and Wendy made their fateful entry into The Museum of Death. Almost everything was still identical to how things were back during their honeymoon. Any changes could be plainly spotted by a prior visitor as most of the rooms were disturbing enough to make an impact.

There was a handful of new animal skeletons that could be viewed upon entry and also an updated picture of Charles Manson, looking quite long in the tooth, in the famous murders room. They'd also added an interesting new display that presented the complete timeline of the evolution of execution methods in America.

The last change was a bit more muted though and was probably the least obvious refinement of the lot. They were still showing the same film Travis and Wendy had trouble trying to stomach, "Happy to Live, Born to Die." The one that sent people running for the door while slipping in their own vomit. The one that presented archival film of horrible accidents, suicides, and without fail, the long-winded footage of the adolescent girl being cracked open.

But if you looked closely, at just the right moment, you would notice a new scene sandwiched within the array of other repugnant events. One would be hard-pressed to recall the new vile footage as it didn't exactly stand out amongst the rest of the mayhem shown in the theater. It was all collectively just so unsettling.

But if you waited long enough at the end of the film, you'd be treated to a short snippet of a girl in a glass case immobilized. Her limbs twisted in a manner that the human form didn't permit as each was caved in backwards at the joints. Her spine had also been partially pulled out and reinserted through her back, exiting below her shoulder.

A decapitated peacock sat in her blood-pooled lap; the spine inserted at a downward angle into the pheasant corpse. In a way, though most wouldn't admit it, the cherry fluid still leaking out of the woman's body looked almost artfully drizzled over the peacock's magnificent coat.

If that wasn't nasty enough, her eyes had gone missing, appearing to have been eaten away in miniature bites. It seemed self-evident that it was the result of the jumbo frothing vulture that was enclosed in the display with her.

The bird looked as if it was inflated by the most

unnatural of methods. Many feathers had gone missing and were replaced by an irritated, scraped-up skin. The bubbly saliva and blood-shot bulging eyes left people wondering why there weren't asylums for birds. They'd rather think of anything than watch the vulture slowly peck the eyes out of the girl's skull, then move onto the lips and nose.

By the time they moved on from the appalling segment, her whole face was massacred. You would think the creature would have had its fill by now but this was an abnormally large bird that never seemed satisfied.

Many of those who couldn't make it through the full sequence either left altogether or made up some kind of excuse to exit and escape for a few moments at the very least.

Considering the restrooms were relatively close and advertised just before the entrance to the theater, it was only natural that a decent demographic would tell their significant others they needed to excuse themselves and use the restroom.

When they finally made it down the stretch of hallway, they would always seem to notice (and some of them even asked about) the exhibit that displayed a sign to patrons of the MOD. No matter how many times one had visited, the sign's status remained unaltered. It was as if Mr. Doctor's Oddities would forever be "Still Under Construction."

DID THEY
DESERVE IT?

Rex had no idea what to do next, he'd never seen a dead body before. Not to mention someone he'd personally known for years. He stood over her petite figure, naked, stewing in a mixture of sweat and shock while he stared down vacantly.

The shiny latex BDSM mask covered most of her face outside of her freshly blackened eyeholes. The chin region zipper was also frayed open, leaving her morbidly-shaded cotton candy lips exposed. The once tender mouth fencing was now cracked and swollen, demonstrating the signature of a new extreme. An extreme that he had never planned on achieving, but nonetheless arrived at.

The rest of her body was also encapsulated in the strict latex, completing the cliché submissive slave ensemble. The only exceptions to the exposure rule applied to both her ass and vaginal area (for obvious reasons). The pose she struck, from where his feet stood, made her appear like some sort of bizarre humanoid pyramid.

She lay on her side, fragile wrists stretched back to her equally strained ankles and bound firmly together in a way most skeletons wouldn't permit. The thick white twine overlapped in an organized way many times over. The knotting configuration was anything but amateur—undeniably an obsessive, scrupulous construction.

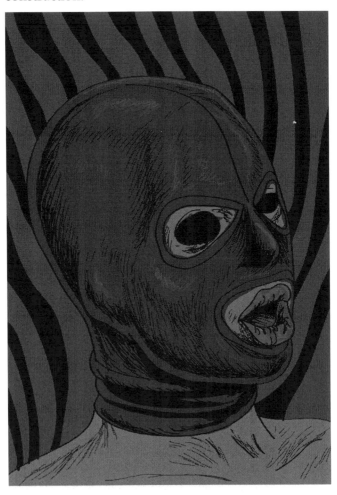

The words "Dumb Slut" were drawn out on her torso in maroon lipstick with a jagged penmanship. She was topped off with dirty, coarse-looking rope that sat coiled around her neck with the other end running up to the ceiling.

Kendra was essentially a booty call, one of the several black book phone numbers he had at his behest. Rex had a problem, but it started a long time before the one that lay contorted in front of him. It was a few years post-puberty when it started to surface. At the time, he considered them disturbing visions, often invading his thoughts without warning, and in some cases, without a trigger.

They ranged from violence against women to humiliation, to asphyxiation, and sometimes worse. They all generated an uncontrollable flavor of excitement that felt forbidden, which, of course, only served to elevate his erection. After great internal effort, he concluded that it was not possible to control the thoughts. He instead decided to just accept and try to ignore them.

That all changed when he met Kendra. Over the course of what started as an innocent friendship, they developed an attraction. Their attraction evolved into infatuation, and before long, Rex learned that Kendra's mind worked a lot like his own.

She helped him unpack his more high-risk, sinister side. A side that Rex was yet to embrace and thought he might never. She gave him a door to exercise the indecencies he was endlessly engulfed in. It felt unreal to have that outlet after so many years of subdual. They joined in a dimension that doesn't display for everyone… indeed, to his experience, it was quite rare.

He knew Kendra was a keeper, realizing that

encountering another person as equally twisted probably wasn't possible. Everything that aroused him and what she found alluring was profoundly out of bounds compared to main-stream lovemaking practices.

They required each other's acquired tastes to pair with their own sinful strain of perversion. The level of deviancy they dug into was a lonely place, so needless to say Rex felt blessed to have her on call. He likened her to a car—old, reliable, always gives me a ride, and never causes any problems.

For all intents and purposes, he'd been right. Even though she presented a highly complex problem presently, it wasn't her aim for him to arrive there. It was never in her control; it was his own doing. A deadly combination of oversight, egotism, and compulsion and just like that, she'd gone stiff…

Their parallel attitudes pushed boundaries but all of the acts they performed together they agreed upon; dissent was almost non-existent. Her past showed in the bedroom. It was clear she'd put some work in. She carried a sort of sexual wisdom that takes decades (if ever) for one to achieve. Those qualities could never be discounted when judging her value.

She might not have been the most beautiful girl but her experience and liberalism scored major points for what he wanted her for. Her body was more than you could ask for, but her narrow, pointed face had earned her the unique nickname of "The Ferret" among friends. Making her wear the mask helped a lot, it also allowed him to make videos and even post them online while still suppressing their identities.

It was 2007, the behavior they engaged in was further out of the closet and more accepted than ever.

Words like choke, bite, spit, slap, pull, rip, bind, and strangle were no longer such veiled taboos.

They could now be found with predictability in many internet browser search histories. For Rex, it really all just tied back to one problem, and it had nothing to do with what lens society viewed his actions through.

Rex was married, going on three years now, and as if that wasn't enough, his wife, Laura, was expecting. It didn't take long for the mid-life crisis blues to start serenading his skull. His mental cage was self-conjured but crept up on him in a slow unobvious way.

He used to be much more available for his deceitful side flings but they were becoming scarcer by the hour. He only realized the web he'd fallen into once he'd already been completely ensnared in it.

The escalation was rapid for such a short timeframe, going from, "Sure, I'd love to go out sometime," to "I'm pregnant" before their first lease was up. Now they were looking for houses and footy pajamas before he'd had a chance to ponder what it was he was even seeking.

From zero to a hundred and the brake-lines were severed and bleeding. In a way, it was terrifying but hardly as terrifying as the motionless corpse on the zebra rug beneath him. He quickly realized he needed to stop thinking about how he got there and focus on how to get out.

He didn't mean to kill her, of course, this was a mutual act of pleasure gone horribly awry. How would that translate in a courtroom though, would they understand? His character would likely cast an unsympathetic shadow from the jump given the circumstances, not to mention the absurdity of the truth itself. He began to run through some of the difficult facts in his mind, in a best-case scenario kind of way, assuming with the prosecution's spin he could even get that far.

FACT: You've been having an extramarital affair with the woman you "accidentally" killed for the entirety of your relationship behind your PREGNANT wife's back.

Right off the rip, that was a real bad look. He would be labeled a cheater, which by default made him a liar. They could tie this unfavorable perception back to anything, at any point to discredit his word. This was more than a character flaw and would help a jury hate him, not trust him.

FACT: Your mistress enjoyed being hung by the neck from a makeshift ceiling pulley, while you sat in a chair below guiding her body up and down during intercourse.

This one was a tough sell but some of Kendra's life choices and possessions may support this. They were, after all, at HER house. It was, after all, HER ceiling lynch. They would find her toy chest and understand that this wasn't her first time around the block. No, sir, she was a professional pervert.

At the same time, that would be some uncomfortable evidence for a defense to present. He pictured his attorney holding a pink rubber dong in a plastic bag and winced. The awkwardness causing a horde of crinkled brows in uniform from the imaginary seated deciders. Hopefully, it wouldn't come off as them grasping at straws or worse, smearing the dead...

On the other hand, he was sure there would be dudes from the past that would surface and be able to cosign on her twisted kinkiness and corroborate her nymphomania. Tie them in with the toy collection, plus a couple of her videos and he might be in business. He was sure if she had videos with other men. He took a side step toward her closet, then thought better of it. This was no time for a movie marathon, he needed to keep thinking.

FACT: You did not intentionally kill her.

The prosecution could easily frame this one how they pleased. Over the years, Kendra had pleaded with him countless times to be exclusive. When he got married, she was heartbroken but would still obey Master Rex above all else.

There's no way to dodge a lifetime of womanizing. The footprints extended far beyond just her and he knew the investigators would be up his ass like a proctologist on his 40th birthday. They don't miss things of that nature, unfortunately for him. It was undeniable, he'd repeatedly used her at his disposal. Kendra felt like trash but she was really more like recycle. She probably had a diary or friend she vented to about it. Not good.

Also not good was the electronic paper trail between them through the years. His wife knew nothing about computers, which, in turn, gave him an ideal secret communication outlet. For years, he exposed his nasty side virtually, the sick concepts all captured in addition to the scheduling of all his various adultery appointments (his favorite, Kendra, included).

He'd seen a few shows about emails being leveraged against people in court cases. Some of their discussions would not be easy to explain. Their messages would also show that even during the time that Laura was pregnant, Kendra was still hounding him to leave her. She commonly spoke with a certain amount of vitriol toward her that he dismissed as jealousy. They would twist that and coach the jury to perceive it as a motive.

FACT: Best case scenario, you get manslaughter.

Manslaughter (which looked like scratch ticket odds at this point), as best he could figure still probably carried at least a five to eight-year prison sentence if he was lucky. Murder, if deemed premeditated, could have him looking at the chair.

Slice it any way you like, it still ruins his life, it still ruins the lives of his family. But was there another way? Was there a way that he could make all of it disappear? Where he could come out unscathed and avoid being eaten alive by the thought of his own culpability? Maybe so, but probably not.

Rex was just a normal guy (psychosexual behavior aside), he didn't really have the stomach for all this morbid shit. But the fright of an unknown, nevertheless assuredly grim future seemed to be smothering his ethics. The kill or be killed mentality was starting to take hold of him. He needed help, he didn't have the stones or the mindset to finish something so fiendish solo.

Fortunately, everyone has that one friend who's a little different. The one you were always afraid to ask what the worst thing they ever did was. The one who just might have some experience with dead bodies.

Trent sat at the edge of his couch fully captivated, entranced by the flickering glow of the television screen. It wasn't fun being a Dolphins fan as of late. Their ten consecutive losses (not to particularly talented teams) made him seriously consider if it was possible for them to win a game this season. Going 0-16 was highly irregular, never having occurred in a sixteen-game season at that point.

The only other team to score losses exclusively for the entirety of a season was the '76 Tampa Bay Buccaneers. Back then, the season only consisted of fourteen games though, so if Miami remained winless, they would give birth to a new echelon of egregious.

Would that be their fate this year? Why did the curse appear to be regulated to teams in the sunshine state? That stench was reserved for a special kind of sucking, he prayed the dubious notion wouldn't be associated with his team.

Ricky Williams had just made his comeback that night but got popped violently on his first run and fumbled. The defensive lineman accidentally stepped on his chest while he laid disoriented, leaving him injured, AGAIN.

This was particularly heartbreaking news in the sense that a victory was somehow easily within grasp. Even against a talented Pittsburg team that, on paper, they had no chance in hell against, they remained scoreless late into the fourth quarter.

The weather may have been a factor as buckets poured down relentlessly. The now nearly extinct natural grass field surface was so drenched that it could almost be classified as a mud pool. All the players were tasked with the extra challenge of fighting for footing on every snap. Just a few minutes prior, a punt hit the ground without bouncing. Instead, it stuck directly into the muck, pointing straight up. In all his years of watching football, he'd never seen anything like it.

Trent noticed a pair of headlights flicker off his trailer window like a car was pulling up. The rain pouring down almost mirrored the streams dropping on the television in Pittsburg. He reached under the coffee table, seizing the revolver from its concealed bat-like hanging position.

Checking the cylinder, he certified he had six slugs loaded before spinning the slut shut. He was ready to rock 'n roll right when he heard a knock at the door.

"If they come a-knockin', they probably ain't no threat," Trent murmured to himself, slipping the gat near his ass crack. He grabbed hold of the door, looking out the cloudy peephole before pulling it open. "Hey, brother! What going on?" Trent asked casually at first.

Rex just stood there soaked, not really knowing what to say. In so many ways, his posture and vibe told Trent something was horribly wrong. He stepped back away from the door offering a lane for Rex to escape from the harsh elements.

"C'mon in, man! What the hell's the matter?"

Rex stepped over the threshold and into the humid trailer's living area. Trent closed the door behind him still trying to figure him out. Was this some kind of joke? Rex was known to be a prankster at times.

"Well? I know you ain't no mute, spit it out," Trent persisted.

"No, I'm…" Rex replied before exhaling deeply, still seeming to not accept it all.

His breathing pattern jumped to a more intense pace as if the air was a commodity that would soon be running out for him.

"I'm in some trouble, Trent," he finally managed.

"Okay, okay, well ain't nothing we can't figure out. Relax, we'll take care of it," Trent replied with a pampering tone and confidence solidifying his statement.

"I'm in big fucking trouble. I don't even wanna tell you, man. I—I don't wanna get you involved in this shit too," he said, nearly hyperventilating.

"I find trouble, trouble don't find me. You can tell me," he replied, attempting to make Rex feel a little more at ease.

Trent had always been like a really cool big brother to him. Never told him what to do but always had his back to the fullest, and if Trent had your back, you were set.

When they met in high school, Trent was a couple of years his senior. He could have a mean streak at times but rarely was it necessary for him to show it... unless you crossed him.

He'd seen him have his fair share of brawls and most were usually justifiable. At the time, to Rex, he was a man without faults, someone to look up to in a lot of ways. He didn't see it in the beginning but neither did anyone else, most probably still didn't. But time has a way of telling you a person's full story if you hang around them enough. He was beginning to understand everyone (himself included) has a dark side. Some just a darker shade than others. He'd had his first glimpse at Trent's just a few years after they graduated. They'd been living together at the time, on a small farm that a friend of theirs owned. They would have all-night ragers where the drugs and booze were bottomless and the promiscuous chicks were topless.

For some reason, a girl that attended the party (who was a mother but obviously not in the true nurturing spirit of the word) chose to bring her child. The three-year-old girl stumbled about harmlessly enough, watching adults do things that they shouldn't until they got further toward the end of the night.

Trent's dog at the time, Polo, had already had his dish filled up about 10 times with beer before he encountered the little girl. She must have pulled his tail or something because he snapped at her, bloodying the tot's face. Her "mother" made a huge scene, screaming at Trent before storming off like a sour cunt and allowing the party to resume.

Trent was overtaken by a menacing seriousness before asking Rex to leash Polo and bring him out back into the cornfield with him. Far away from the party, Rex watched as Trent produced a large serrated hunting knife while Polo began to whimper. The dog stared up at him almost like it had known for some time that day was inevitable.

Without hesitation, he stabbed the dog over and over ruthlessly. The sound of the steel running through his meat and muscle mixed with his piercing cries and trance music in the background was sickening.

Rex found it astonishing how decisive and cruel he was. A dog he had cared for, for over 5 years, he completely destroyed in a matter of minutes. He'd never seen Trent act in such a numb manner before or after that night. The circumstances didn't excuse his actions. The image of the butchered pup was still burned into his memory like it happened yesterday.

Poor Polo's behavior didn't warrant the brand of malice he'd received. It made Rex sick at the time but he was too fearful to object. That night, he walked away with a new understanding of Trent's capabilities.

Looking back on it, in a warped way, it was a good thing it occurred. The deed was disgusting but if he hadn't witnessed it, he might not have anyone to get him through tonight. The flashback helped persuade him to explain.

"You remember that girl we all used to fuck? Kendra?" Rex asked.

"Kendra, Kendra… Kennnnddrrrraaa. Not really ringing a bell," he said, pondering aloud.

"She lived in Oak Lawn with Cindy?"

"Kendra?"

"She looked like a ferret?"

"Oh! The ferret! Yeah, man, right on. You shoulda just said the fuckin' ferret, no one calls her Kendra," he said with a laugh as Rex's eyes started to tear up.

"No. Don't tell me you got her pregnant! That bitch is a dumpster fire, Rex, I'm telling you. You better have her get rid of that. She ain't the kinda woman you'd wanna be attached to for 18 years," Trent said, getting worked up. Rex began to sob, slumping down on the couch. Trent sat down beside him feeling like he was missing something.

"Does Laura know? That's why you're upset? She found out you knocked up the ferret? That's it, right?"

Rex shook his head subtly from side to side. Trent looked over to the TV. Only seventeen seconds left and Pittsburg's kicker was now lining up for a 24-yarder that could end the game. He'd been trying to give Rex his full attention but he was really dragging it out. He'd already politely suppressed some of the fury that bubbled after viewing a large completion on the potential game-winning drive.

"What is it?" he said, a bit louder and more impatient.

Not taking his eyes off the screen, he held his breath. The kick went up rotating continuously in what felt like slow motion. The kick was good. Trent shot up off of the couch and flipped the small yellow coffee table effortlessly. Papers flew up and empty bottles hit the floor.

"Fuuuuuuuuck! Piece of shit team! Bunch of losers, I hope you all fucking die, I hope each of yo—"

"Kendra's dead!" Rex blurted out finally.

The words tranquilized Trent, realizing quickly the game no longer meant anything. He slowly descended back to his seat, snatching up the remote that was now on the floor beside him. He switched off the television before turning to Rex.

"I'm sorry, maybe I didn't hear that right. Come again?"

"She's dead. She's dead and I killed her," Rex confirmed, voice trembling.

"You're kidding! Ha, you're really good. So serious, man, you make it feel real."

Rex began to choke up again, living the nightmare. As much as he wanted it to be, Trent was now seeing this was clearly no joke.

"W-why'd you kill her, Rex? I mean, did she deserve it at least?" Trent stammered, dumbfounded by the revelation.

"Of course not! It was an accident. It happened at her house when we were having sex. You know her, man, you know she likes it rough. She asked me to… to choke her. SHE. ASKED. ME. I had her neck tied to the asphyxiation pulley she made, I musta… I musta held her up too long. She liked it, she liked it, man, I swear," Rex cried.

"Whoa, this is some David Carradine type shit we're getting into here. What I don't understand is why you're telling me, you gotta call the police, Rex. Tell me you called the police."

"The police!? Man, I can't call the police, they're

gonna give me the fuckin' chair. How do you expect them to believe me, you hardly believed me! This is some fantastical shit we're talking about! I've got a pregnant wife at home, they're gonna say it was intentional. You know how they spin these things."

"But it wasn't."

"Even if it wasn't, on the off chance my dollar store defense attorney can prove that, it's still manslaughter. It's still prison. Trent, you know as well as I know they'd eat me alive in prison. I'm just not built for that life. It would be game over for me."

They both paused. Trent sat back on the couch and squinted his eyes at Rex. "So, what are you askin' me?"

"I'm asking for this to disappear. I'm asking to keep my life and not destroy my family over something that was an accident. You know me, I could never do this. I need your help, Trent, you're all I got."

"Enough with the fuckin' riddles, Rex. I'm not Houdini, things don't just disappear. Are you asking me to help dump a body?"

Rex nodded his head disgracefully.

"If there is no body, there is no crime, or at least it's a lot less likely, right? There is no evidence of violence, I just showed up at her place tonight, I didn't call her or anything. No one even knows I was there. There would be a laundry list of other fuck friends to consider before me."

"I'd say so. What about her family? I mean, we both know her brother for Christ sake. Nick is an old friend, is he gonna have to live the rest of his life wondering where his sister is?"

"Better than knowing she died hanging from her ceiling while getting fucked! This could save her family some shame and still give them a little hope, even if it's false hope."

"Jesus," Trent scoffed.

"Look, I don't have all the answers but I don't wanna die. If you got a better idea I'm all fuckin' ears! Otherwise, I'm begging you to help me," Rex pleaded.

"Why me? Why you gotta throw this shit on me?" Trent asked.

"Because I know you can handle it."

They pulled around the back of Kendra's trailer attempting a stealthy entry. Thankfully, she lived on a private lot with about a half-mile buffer zone. They just had to worry about people driving down the seldomly used road.

Parking around back would guarantee no one would be able to finger Rex's vehicle. Luckily, Rex always parked out back to avoid people he knew placing him there, so his earlier visit wouldn't be an issue either. He didn't want word that he was up to something shady getting back to Laura from a nosy passerby.

The boys got out, surrounded by the patter of rainfall smacking against the nearby vegetation. Rex had left her back door ajar in hopes that he might convince Trent to return with him, thankfully, that was the case.

They stepped through the threshold, entering the dimly lit room. Rex again comprehended the severity of his actions and Trent tried to digest them for the first time. It was plainly obvious, the stupidity of the scenario irked him. He could feel the realness setting in but tried to maintain his cool.

"Jesus, this is some... you watch way, WAY too

much porno, man. I, I can't believe you done this." Trent barked in a low, aggravated tone.

"I know, dammit! I know I screwed up big!"

"Screwed up? You call this a screw-up? You turn the ferret into a goddamn latex pretzel and that's what you call it?!" Trent cried.

Interrupting his rant was a loud banging on the front door about 15 feet away from them. Alarm paralyzing them both, they looked at each other like their guts had fallen out. How could it be? They'd literally just arrived, had someone tailed them?

"Who the fuck is that now?!" Trent squawked, whispering his rage.

"How the hell should I know? You know how promiscuous she is…" Rex responded.

"Maybe they'll just leave if we're quiet."

Rex's theory proved inaccurate when they heard the worst possible noise someone in their shoes could hope for… the sound of a key being inserted into a lock and slowly popping it open.

They'd both retreated back toward the bedroom, peering through the curtain of beads used to separate the rooms.

Trent used his hand to try and steady them, knowing only something terrible could happen now. That individual could only be there for one reason and the reason was in a much different state than they would normally be accustomed to.

"Kendraaaaaaaa," the voice called out, hitting an eleven on the Creep-O-Meter.

The man was wearing a tightly fastened pink silk robe, a mask which very realistically portrayed the face of a male child, and filthy boots that appeared to have just ran a marathon through a field of shit.

"The boy is baaaaack now," the figure said, turning himself toward her twisted frame. "Look at you, you're all ready for me ahead of schedule. That's my girl," he said, opening up his robe.

"He's gonna find out, we gotta confront him now," Trent whispered.

"Confront him and then what?" Rex retorted.

"I don't know but he's gonna figure it out, Rex! We gotta act, not react here," he said, pulling the revolver from the crack of his ass.

"Oh, don't wanna talk to me today? That's okay. We don't need to talk," the creep said, sitting down in the chair in front of her.

"You're crazy! What you're talking about is murder here!" Rex tried to reason.

"Keep your fuckin' voice down! I gotta get the jump on him," Trent commanded with a "don't fuck with me or I'll bury you with him" sort of look spiraling around in his eye.

"Trent. You're making a BIG mistake that you can't take back."

The creep was now elevating Kendra off the ground, tugging at the pulley. She was once again dangling and almost at his eye level.

"You brought me into this, it was your call. You knew I was a wild card. This is my ass now too," Trent reminded him.

The creep now sat eyes locked with Kendra and it was overly apparent that something was dead wrong. Her lips and flesh discolored, no sign of breathing or any noise, and she hadn't blinked yet…

"What the fuc—"

Trent was done listening, he stepped out through the bead curtain with the burner drawn. At first, Rex grabbed at him, attempting to hold him back but he was no match for Trent's power, he pushed him off effortlessly sending him flying onto a pile of VHS tapes. He crashed hard and must have landed on the remote because it activated the TV set.

Trent wrapped his arm around the creep's throat from behind, pressing the barrel to his cranium, cutting short his muddled train of thought.

"Alright, fuck boy, hands in the air before I spray your brains all over your little playdate here. Turn around and you die."

The creep let go of the rope tied to Kendra and her corpse rushed down, bouncing off him before toppling over onto the zebra rug.

"Who are you, man? I was just here, I just, I just came to see her, man. I swear it!" the creep pleaded.

"Well, unfortunately, what we have here is a little case of wrong place wrong time," Trent explained, grinding the gun against his skull.

"I won't say shit, man, I swear. Kendra was just a whore, a filthy bitch. I'm not going to put your life or mine in jeopardy."

"No, you're certainly not." Tent loosened his chokehold.

He stood back up behind him, still with the gun leveled at the back of his head.

"Lose the fucking mask," Trent said.

"I haven't seen your face, I still don't even know who you are, man. Let's just keep it that way," the creep begged.

"If I gotta tell you again, you won't have to worry about seeing my face, you'll be seeing your own all over the fuckin' floor." The threat seemed to resonate. He pulled the mask off to reveal a rumbled bundle of black hair—greasy and unkempt. "I don't wanna repeat myself again. Turn around." The creep turned around as a look of disbelief overtook Trent's face.

"Nick?! What the fuck are you doing here?!" Trent cried, the pit of his stomach sinking.

"Trent?! What? I knew that voice was familiar. I just couldn't place it."

"You fuckin' your sister, Nick?"

"That's a fair question… but did you, did you kill my sister, Trent?"

"Treeeennt! Get in here," Rex yelled from the back bedroom.

"Just a second, dammit!"

"Who the fuck is that, Trent? What in God's name is going on here?" Rex hollered through the curtain.

Trent looked to the chair Nick sat in, noticing bondage cuff clamps were built into the perverse device. He leveled the gun at Nick and activated each clamp to keep him subdued.

"C'mon, Trent, we've known each other forever. You, you can't kill me, man."

"Just hang tight a minute for me," he said, taking a few steps back through the beads but still keeping the revolver extended through them.

What he saw next was almost more powerful than the prior shock. If the first one would've killed him, this one would've brought him back to life. On the TV that Rex had accidentally activated played a VHS tape that showed Nick, the twisted sister-fister, and Kendra both beside a man tied to a chair.

He was morbidly obese and his massive body was quivering. They were taking turns blowing him, which at this point would have been disturbing enough, but as Trent's eyes followed the TV screen to the top, he saw the man had no head. The blood was now running down all over their hair as they continued the ungodly performance.

"See if you can still make him cum," Kendra whispered to Nick as he picked up the pace on the shaking body.

"Turn this shit off!" Disgust saturated Trent's words.

Trent drove them into what felt like the deepest, darkest woods imaginable. Rex had allowed him to take the wheel for their drive, he said he knew a place where they would never find them. It was a bit of a hike, they'd been in the car for over an hour, anxiety elevating throughout the duration.

He sure seemed to be onto something, Rex had no idea how Trent was able to navigate the area in the downpour, he fit them through crevasses and between trees that didn't seem achievable at first glance. This wasn't even a road really, more just like driving through the forest.

When they finally pulled over, they came to a minuscule opening within the crowded surrounding forest. It looked like a handful of trees had been cleared out but they barely had enough space to park. They exited the car simultaneously as it stopped.

Trent popped the trunk and they both immediately headed to the rear of the car, snatching up the shovels laid over Nick's tied-up, squirming body and his sister's stiff triangular form. Nick sat up a bit and tried to speak, though the ball gag prohibited him. Trent paid him no mind, slamming the trunk down and banging his head violently as it closed.

"I think the best spot is probably over here, the ground is a little bit softer," he said, pointing to the left of the car.

A curious yet timid look crossed Rex's face. "How'd you know that? I mean, how'd you find out about this place?" Rex prodded.

"This is where I buried Polo, Rex. You remember Polo, don't you?" Trent asked.

"Yeah, that's right, Polo. How could I forget?"

The two started digging, putting down sloppy scoops of muck to the far outskirts of the hole. After about twenty minutes or so, they seemed to be getting close. Two shovels were much better than one. Rex was quite grateful that Trent had a couple at his house. He felt so lucky to have someone helping, he wouldn't even know where to begin with something like this.

The long drive and seeing the evil things that Nick had done with his sister on the VHS made him feel less guilty about Kendra's demise and how Nick's fate was set to unfold. He wished he could wash his hands completely of the series of events but some things were just irreversible.

"Looks like we're about done here," Rex remarked.

"Just a little more, we have to make sure we get down six feet so the animals don't get to 'em," Trent replied.

"Boy, you sure are very knowledgeable, Trent. I don't know what I'd do without you."

"Don't think nothing of it."

"You know, this is gonna sound really fucked-up, but I'm glad we found it."

"Glad we found what?" Trent wondered.

"I'm glad we found the tape. I mean, remember

earlier at your house, you asked me flat out if she deserved it… at the time, I thought no way in hell she did. But after that tape, there's no doubt in my mind."

"Yeah, that was something else alright."

"I mean, I still feel horrible, I do, but now at least I know. I know they deserved it, Trent," Rex said, looking up at his partner through the rainstorm sounding truly convinced.

After about another ten minutes, they'd finally finished. There was so much water the hole was a partially filled pool but it was hard to tell since it looked like a bottomless pit in the moonlight.

Trent extended his hand and helped Rex hop out of the pit. He made his way back to the vehicle and grabbed hold of Kendra's stiffening corpse. Trent dragged Nick out next. They lugged the pair of incestual siblings over to the hole. Nick was completely bound but still put up a spirited struggle.

Rex tossed Kendra's body into the watery grave without hesitation. A minor splash could be heard kicking around the liquid on the muddy floor. Trent then turned to Rex almost waiting for him to say something but Rex had no idea what he needed to say.

"You wanna do the honors?" Trent asked, removing the revolver from his jacket and spinning the cylinder.

"Umm..." Rex hesitated.

"That's okay, it's your first time. I can see you've got the jitters. It's not a problem, Rex."

"Of course, it's my first time, man! This is your first time too, right?"

Lightning struck without warning. It felt like it wasn't too far from them, illuminating the sky and their backdrop. For a split second, it revealed what looked to be numerous grave plots all across the rear of the open area. At least Rex thought that's what he saw, it was so quick but so impactful he began to question himself internally.

Trent quickly used his leg to lean Nick back a bit as he fidgeted on his knees, squeezing the trigger without thought. The bullet blew the top of his wig back, exposing a soup of blood and chunks underneath. The momentum from being shot sent him somersaulting backward, landing on top of his sister, his brains spilling out over her stiff cadaver.

The abrupt, malevolent action made Rex jump. He continued to tremble after the initial shock, mostly over the thought that it seemed way too natural for Trent.

"I hope your sister's pussy was worth it, faggot," Trent said before spitting on them both.

"Alright, let's bury them and get the fuck out of here," Rex stammered, grabbing the shovel and starting to fling mud over their bodies immediately.

"Just hold on a second now, Rex. Didn't you notice? I made that grave a little wider than we needed. There's room for one more in there," Trent said just before shooting Rex in the kneecap.

Rex fell into the soaked mud, screaming. The filthy water cascading over his cheeks. He grabbed his joint, applying pressure to the leaking wound.

"You shot me! You fucking shot me!" he shrieked.

"Well, but that's okay, Rex. You deserved it, didn't you? You're responsible for killin' a woman tonight. Given she probably wasn't exactly a pillar of the community or anything, but still. Guilty of cheating on your wife and hell, throw in being a shitty friend for dragging me into this mess."

"You fucking psychopath!" Rex mustered.

"Maybe, but I can tell you everyone I ever killed deserved it. Every person I laid down on these grounds was hurting people. They were selfish, sick people. They were all evil as the day is long. They had a disease of the mind. You can't work on that kind of issue, Rex. There was no saving them."

At that moment, mid-speech, Trent pulled an all too familiar serrated hunting knife which only escalated Rex's distress. His whines sounded a lot like the whimpers Polo released that night in the field and he surely had the same look in his eyes.

"All these people," Trent said, pointing the knife about as a second bolt of lightning struck in the distance, illuminating the countless gravesites.

"It all started with that dog. That dog made me realize that I was put here with a higher purpose in mind. Before long, I expect to fill up this whole place."

FACT: Trent stabbed you fifteen times before dumping your body into the cold grave with the others. At the time, though there was no way he could have known, it would be one stab for every loss the Miami Dolphins would earn that year.

*FUN FACT: The 2007 Miami Dolphins lone victory would come on a 64-yard overtime throw against the Baltimore Ravens on which Cleo Lemon connected with Greg Camarillo. He became a hero at least for a week by helping Miami avoid what would have been, at the time, the only winless season by a team in the era of the 16-game schedule. In addition, that season they would also become the first NFL team to lose overseas, falling to the eventual Super Bowl Champion New York Giants by a score of 13-10.

THE BREAKDOWN

Donna had never dreamed she'd be in the position she found herself in. The brutal chill of the Minnesota air further froze her already icy blood flow. On the 18th of January 1996, winter hit the town of Tower with an uncanny cruelty. This record-setting stretch was so brutal, it had historical implications.

The run was filled with constant storms and certain times of the day saw the temperature falling as far as 60 degrees below zero. The ordinarily peaceful haven that so many residents always took for granted was now more hazardous than just about anywhere else in the country.

Earlier in the week, they'd already lost one local due to the extraordinary conditions. Thomas Kelp, the owner of a local gas station, was discovered frozen in his car on the desolate Great Mile Road. The radio reported that he'd broken down and must have been waiting in hopes someone would pass by. There he sat cold and hopeful, but with each minute that passed his spirit and confidence dwindled.

Kelp had decided to stay in his vehicle rather than walking, putting his chances of survival in the hands of a passerby. Unfortunately for Thomas, all the townsfolk were more than mindful of the imminent peril the conditions presented, as any proud Minnesotan would be.

A plow truck driver would eventually stumble upon the situation, Kelp's car partially buried on the side of the road, the faint flicker of the breakdown lights triggering him to investigate. The windows were still a little foggy when he pulled on the door handle. He found Thomas motionless, frozen solid with his eyes sealed shut.

It appeared his life had concluded while drifting into a chilling slumber. His body slowly shut down, arms outstretched as if he was still attempting to drive away in the dead vehicle. Paramedics were eventually given the grim task of breaking each of his fingers in order to pry them off the steering wheel.

That was the only image Donna could reflect upon while sitting in her truck, absent of heat and every ordinarily taken for granted amenity. She didn't even have the luxury of listening to the radio and the unyielding warnings that were being disseminated over the air waves, which she'd failed to heed.

"This weather warning has been issued so you can start to take precautions from the dangerous cold, frostbite can happen in under 10 minutes," was the last time she'd heard a human voice. Although it was distorted and less warm as it escaped the crackly speakers, it was still comforting at the time, but now, it just felt cryptic.

The words continued to swirl in her mind, she couldn't seem to dissuade herself to sway from the concept that it was highly probable that she'd end up just as cold and just as dead as Mr. Kelp. She already regretted initiating her foolish excursion, but love will make you do irrational things.

It was only fitting the day that would be remembered for the worst blizzard in Tower's existence was the day she chose to call her recently relabeled ex-boyfriend, Roy, out on his shit. Being trapped with him the past few days had made her a bit stir crazy; her accusatory conspiracies repetitively poisoned her thoughts without fail.

She confronted him over a handful of condoms she'd found in his jacket earlier in the afternoon. Of course, he denied it, calling her a "crazy, nosy bitch" and seemed like he was a few more exchanges away from smacking her. The argument ensued in a more cautious manner on her end, followed by her finally mustering the courage to cut bait on what she finally realized to be a rotten, deceptive relationship.

The move was long-overdue and she felt a sense of pride and refreshment stirring inside her. However, the wondrous sense of freedom and independence was quickly forgotten once she realized how treacherous the drive was.

Layer upon layer of ice under her tires, mounds of towering snow, and an aggressive cold had caused her a shocking amount of pain on the relatively short walk to her truck. She couldn't bear to be around the bastard though, no matter what risk she faced as a result of her rage fueled choice.

Her mother's house was only about twelve miles away from Roy's. She convinced herself she could make it, but a lurking terror remained pulsating slightly, in a dormant state at the moment…

It didn't reach full force until she was about five miles out, the point of no return so to speak. The normally reliable engine was suffocated by the wicked winter's grasp, the struggle to keep running was the absolute last sound she wanted to hear. At this point, she would have even preferred Roy's uneducated "know-it-all-when-you-don't-know-shit" tone. Almost anything would be better than her current status.

As the car rolled to a stop on the shoulder of the road near a snowbank, the heat died out, along with the peaceful country guitar strumming that she'd been ignoring for the better part of the ride. This weather had already killed one engine and it was all over the news specifically to warn people like her. She scolded herself, knowing she'd made possibly the most idiotic decision of her life.

She tried turning it over a few dozen times but something was horribly wrong. She was no mechanic but absolutely nothing was working. She knew the next few decisions she would make would determine her fate, whether she'd have a chance to be a mother like she'd always wanted, or die cold and alone like she'd always feared. It was already chilly in the car, the small bit of heat that was circulating had quickly disappeared. It was decision time now.

In a town of maybe 500 people, she had to break down in the worst possible area. Roy lived near the water and her mom was in the city—the only thing that separated the two areas was a few lonely roads within a giant patch of country.

So, would she wait and pray someone was foolish enough to venture outside, ignoring the numerous warnings plastered between every song on the radio? Or would she get out and walk?

She'd be lucky to keep her fingers and toes if she did. She estimated it would be well over five miles on very difficult footing to reach any sort of housing. There were houses sporadically placed throughout the woods that she'd seen but she didn't spend much time in that area of town. No one did really unless you lived out that way.

She felt the cold viciously gnawing into her, paralyzing her. She was beginning to sense weariness clinging onto her. If she was going to have a shot at surviving this, she'd have to move now, while she was relatively energized still. She was leaning toward betting that no one was going to be as emotional and decisive as she was today.

No one could be insane enough to leave their house in what was perhaps the most precarious conditions in the history of Tower. If they did, it sure as hell wouldn't be on this stretch of road, Mr. Kelp could confirm that much. She felt it was in her best interest not to follow in his footsteps or lack thereof. She opened the truck door, absolving herself of any outstanding doubt. In her eyes, it was time to move or die.

It didn't take long for her to completely lose the feeling of her fingertips and toes. A bluish hue manifested over the numb areas; her skin now waxy to the touch. Her terror grew with each step seeming more difficult than the prior one.

She'd been walking for what must have been almost a mile when she was presented the next choice. She could stay on Great Mile Road, knowing she would have to make it at least another four miles before she saw any housing, or she could roll the dice. Take a left down the seldom-used Solomon Road, which she'd never even heard of.

Tears drizzled about a third of the way down her face before slowing to a freeze. She took a deep breath doing an exceptional job of suppressing the panic that most average citizens would undeniably be allowing to blur their better judgment. It was circumstances like this where you could learn things about yourself that you otherwise might never come to comprehend. You find out who you really are.

Evidently, Donna was a fighter. Her usually girly, princess persona was now nowhere to be found. In the bat of an eye, that version was dead and she'd unknowingly skipped the funeral. She hadn't even put any thought into it, it just kind of happened organically. Sometimes, in order to survive, you have to be reborn.

Donna was in full-on survival mode, shifting into a gear she didn't even know she had. She didn't take gloves or a hat so she had to use her hood and pockets as best she could. Even with her thick, feathery winter jacket, she knew that she didn't have much time before she'd be at risk of frostbite.

Already, she felt like she'd recognized some of the early symptoms setting in, again utilizing a mysterious, previously inactive instinct. She knew there was an incredibly small window before her body would be subject to irreparable damages or worse, and this window was closing fast.

Her hesitation evaporated, she began to ascend the slight incline onto Solomon Road. If she was going to survive, she knew this was the path she'd need to walk. She began to pray to God, out loud at first but quickly substituted the vocal aspect. Instead, she prayed inside her head in an effort to ration her vigor and breath.

They were just old prayers burned into her memory from her childhood days in Catholic school but as she recited them, they reminded her of those warm afternoons inside the classroom. Thinking back to the window she sat by during Morning Prayer, looking out into the frigid temperatures from the confines of her cozy seat.

The warm fuzzy memories did little to fix her predicament. And as she walked, she continued to self-reflect, realizing that these mindless memorized lines would not cut the mustard. She needed to legitimately talk to God, cut to the chase instead of speaking in the same riddles that millions of people drown out multiple times every day. How could God hear her voice if it was in unison with millions of others? No, it didn't make a lick of sense, she needed to send him a unique message that stood out.

"Dear God, it's me, Donna. I know we haven't talked in a while but I think… I think I've been a pretty good person by general moral standards. I've never really wronged anyone in a malicious way, I mean, I'm not perfect but really only your son was, right? I know I don't talk to you often and it probably seems like I'm just calling on you when I need help, but I really need help. I think if I don't find help soon, I'm going to die… And I have things I need to do before I die.

I have to take care of my mom; she's not going to get on easily by herself and I need to make sure Ana grows up okay. My sister, Cheryl, is a good person but she is just not a natural mother, she has to try really hard and I know… I know Ana is going to need me when she's older. I want to be there for her, I have to be there for her… I don't think I've ever asked you for anything but if you think I deserve it, please, please let me see a house soon. Any house at all, I just need to find a house."

Donna didn't even really know if she believed in God but now more than ever, she trusted he existed. She trotted out her newly formed blind faith to the front of her mind and focused. He had to exist, he had to. The more she believed, the better her chances, realizing the power of positivity was a rather profound tool and one of the few, if not the only, at her disposal.

It was time for a pulse check, she thought, extracting her hands from her coat pockets to take a quick look. They'd transitioned from an irritated red frostnip to a bright white color which she could only assume was the next stage of frostbite. Still, the area surrounding her was a whiteout, encompassed by snow feathering its way down gracefully. But unlike the last road, this one had small hills. Small enough so she never knew when she might reach a little peak and see some form of civilization just ahead. This gave her additional hope as she went back to the prayers.

"Please, God, let me find a house. Please, God, let me find a house. Please, God, let me find a house. Please, God, let me find a house! PLEASE, GOD, LET ME FIND A HOUSE! GOD, PLEASE! ANY HOUSE!" she cried through her icy tears.

She fell to the ground in a heap, it seemed like she'd reached some sort of line she had no idea was coming. She was cracking up. The cries twisted to an almost maniacal laughter, followed a seething fury.

"Fuck you, God, you're a piece of shit. You're not real, you're a myth. A children's fable. A fucking pathetic sleeping pill for people with problems so they can get a little shut-eye, convincing themselves you're up there to slow the issues worming through their minds all night. What kind of sick joke are you? What kind of a—"

Her rant of madness was cut short as she spied something that couldn't be possible. Just a few more yards over a small hill, she could see a trail of smoke. Where there's smoke, there's fire. Where there's fire, there's heat. Where there's heat, there's life. Her jaw would have dropped if it wasn't busy being blue and chattering.

"I'm sorry, I was wrong! I love you, God! You're so amazing, I can't believe I didn't trust in you!" she yelled with the jubilation of a lottery winner.

Donna quickly picked herself up off the ground, slipping a bit before gaining her balance and heading full speed over the hill. She could see it now; through the old single-family house's windows, she spied the glow of orangey flames flickering enticingly in the dim afternoon light.

A sigh of immeasurable relief escaped her as she pressed on full speed ahead. She made her way up the slippery stone steps without fail before scuttling up to the white door. A lion's mouth held the knocker which she unflinchingly clenched firmly, banging it about ten times in a desperately aggressive manner.

She heard nothing behind the door, waiting mere seconds before quickly pounding on it again, this time with both fists.

"Hello?! Please, I need help!" she shouted, any sort of calm evaporated.

After the second set, she could hear what she thought were footsteps on the other side of the door. She continued to bang on the door, this time a bit more gently, doing her best not to frighten the occupant. She knew this individual on the other side of the door was likely her last lifeline.

"Hello, please open up, my truck, I—I've broken down a few miles back. I think I'm frostbit; I can't feel my hands or toes."

The door lock turned, which, for her money, was the best, most priceless event of her life. Until she saw what was on the other side...

When the door came fully ajar, she found a large man standing before her. Not just large but soaring.

This was by far the largest man she had ever seen in her life. He was so tall, it bordered on unnatural. His hands could easily cover her face which measured up to his abdomen if the pair were to stand side by side.

His pupils seemed quite large but were shrouded by his overgrown bushy eyebrows and further because they sunk into his skull to an unusual depth. His massive beak-like nose hovered over a long reddish-brown mustache that was the thickness of a cigar. His greasy hair slithered down, out of a winter cap. The Mustache Man stood without reaction.

Now faced with this strange new dynamic, Donna began to stammer. Her words exited her mouth to the same beat of her shivers.

"My, my tr—truck. It broke down. Thank G—God you're here, otherwise, otherwise…" she trailed off.

"Come in," the Mustache Man said in a slurred voice that reeked of mental retardation.

She really had no choice but to step inside. Her options had been simplified. She could either stay with the bizarre man or freeze to death. An easy choice, although the thought that there are things worse than death did cross her mind. She purged that concept from her brain, preparing to take the leap of faith. After all, God had led her there.

As she stepped closer to him, a potent funk forced its way up her nostrils. He was dispersing a smell she'd never encountered before; it could only be likened to something rotten infused with nauseating hygiene. She gagged but quickly caught herself, instead, breathing through her mouth to try and stomach it in a less noticeable manner. The last thing she wanted to do was offend the Mustache Man.

He gestured to a dirty old rocking chair that sat in

front of an aged wood stove. The furniture appeared to be from an era before she existed. Following his instruction, she took a seat, removing her hands from her pockets to hold them in front of the flames.

To her horror, more than half of the fingers on each of her hands had turned pitch black. They were now undoubtedly in a deep frostbite stage, which she knew signified that the tissue was dead and now useless. She had trouble moving them and tried rubbing them as she began to sob. The Mustache Man shifted his gaze to her sobs and laughed. His cackle sounded like a drunk child.

"Seeing the girls will help," he managed.

Donna continued crying and staring at her plagued fingers while the Mustache Man left the room. He returned back with a large stein and handed it to her.

"Drink," he instructed.

Shaking and howling, she grabbed the stein; her tremors were so violent that she spilled some of the steaming liquid on herself. On any other day, the burn would have hurt. Today though, with a more twisted sadistic mindset, she enjoyed the feeling.

She looked into the cup before drinking, untrusting of the man's judgment. Her concerns were clearly warranted, through the steam she could see a brownish liquid swirling as she continued to shake. But what she wondered was if the movement in the liquid was due to her instability or something else…

She didn't want to find out. The complexion of the vile concoction looked and smelled like something that came from the deepest bowels of the sewer. The thought of the Mustache Man's potential primitive reaction if she rejected his offer terrified her, even more so than gulping down the mystery substance.

She decided she would feign taking a sip, letting the foul fluid sit on her top lip for a moment to appease his wishes. As she held the cup, she suddenly felt a sharp piercing bite, causing her to jump and spill some of the contents on her chest. She stood immediately and handed the offering back to him.

"Th—Thank you, thank you so much. That really hit the spot," she managed to stammer out as nonchalantly as possible.

"Seeing the girls will help," he repeated.

"I'm sorry, I'm not sure what you mean?" she replied, blood now trickling down her lips and chin.

"Come," he ordered, gesturing her to follow him as he proceeded to another door at the far end of the house.

Donna obeyed his commands up until they reached the door. When he opened it, a chorus of faint muffled moans danced up the decrepit stairwell. It sounded hellish. The noises that were inaudible—either because of their prior distance or the crackle of the fire—were now all too real.

Her stomach sank, devastation setting in as it was now certain that she had selected a fate worse than freezing to death. She would give anything to be alone right now.

"I think I—I'd rather just stay by the fire. I'm still freezing," she said.

The Mustache Man stared into her eyes from his sunken flesh caves, almost robotic, if a machine could seem evil. He elevated the stein quickly, throwing the putrid liquid in her face, scalding her skin. His massive hands then found their way around the back of her neck as he tossed her with ease down the stairs.

Her tumble beat upon her rigid body, concluding

with her skull smacking against the cold concrete floor. The moans now surrounded her and had hit an earsplitting pitch. She tried to regain her bearings and as Donna lifted her head, she could see what all the commotion was.

The nightmare was real. Any chance that this was a misunderstanding had fled as she fixed eyes on three ravaged girls laying on the basement floor. They all moaned for similar but diverse reasons. Each one was missing different body parts. It looked like a butcher shop down there.

One girl was even missing her whole face. It was substituted with a garbled mess of slick wet flesh, her teeth and gums exposed, positioned in a permanent grimace. This woman also had both feet severed at the ankles; the nubs were raw but somewhat healed.

The next girl was missing both of her hands and one leg from the kneecap down. She sat balancing on her lone limb against the wet walls in the corner. Again, the leg injury appeared healed but the hands were fresh.

The final one was probably the saddest of the lot, just a torso squirming about like fish out of water. A massive pool of blood beneath her made it look like a Hollywood production, an amount seen only in the movies. She splashed around in it but was unable to create much of a disturbance in her current state.

That was the last thing Donna recalled just before everything went dark. She regained consciousness sometime later, finding herself sitting with her coat and shoes off not far from the moaning girls. She looked down and noticed both of her feet were also black, infected with the deep frostbite.

Her stunned gawk continued. Climbing up from her feet, she noticed an unmistakable giant shadow erected motionless in front of her. There was no doubt it was him. He stepped forward, brandishing his same blank expression, colder than the weather she'd sought shelter from.

He held a pair of the largest, sharpest, sturdiest-looking scissors she'd ever seen. These were not some sort of gardening tool; these were something crafted. Something original. Something nefarious.

"I take the black," the Mustache Man confessed.

She tried to scream but nothing came out. He sat on her, using his weight to pin her down and opened the shiny metal device. She flailed and screamed to no avail. The Mustache Man grabbed each hand and used the scissors to cut the blackened, frostbitten parts off of her. When he was finished with her, Donna's hands looked like she'd just pulled the pin out of a grenade and held it too long.

He remained mounted on her but switched positions now, securing her left ankle. The frostbite was up to her lower shinbone, so that is exactly where he cut. She was still trying to scream but the only sounds she could make were on a mousey scale. The dark necrotic flesh fell to the cold ground with a nauseating thud.

He then giddily snatched the other leg which had frostbite halfway up the foot, and again, opened the scissors. This time upon their closure, the mangled female hovering angrily in the corner of the basement pounced on him.

Her handless arms were still oozing a recent red as she plunged her bloodied extremities into the Mustache Man's eyes. His scissors slipped off target, only slicing three toes off Donna's foot instead of the whole lot of dead tissue.

He fell back unexpectedly dropping the scissors. Blinded by the blood that had pooled within his sunken sockets, he swung his elongated limbs violently while the deformed girl wrapped around him.

Throughout the ordeal, Donna had been eyeing a means of escape, regardless of how unrealistic her chances were. She quickly executed her fantasy plan, throwing on her jacket beside her and grabbing a wooden cane-like stick from a cob-web-covered corner of the basement.

While the Mustache Man continued his struggle downstairs, she made her way up them with a speed that any athlete in the Special Olympics would find admirable. She was never sporty really but looked all state currently. Even with her hobble hindering her, she didn't stumble. Fueled by pure adrenaline and the fear that death itself was in the basement, she reached the top of the stairs.

She slammed the door shut on the subdued screams and ruckus, taking one step closer to separating herself from it. She noticed a padlock on the door which she promptly triggered with her quivering mutilated hands. A thought of eagerness inserted itself into her mind as she blew through the front door and fell down the icy steps, dropping her cane. "I get to die alone in the woods," she whispered excitedly to herself, more grateful than ever.

It seemed like such a treat after the dread and torture she'd endured. She had a smirk on her face as she ran deeper into the woods, leaning on the cane and her partially severed foot to distance her from the evil.

After about fifteen or twenty minutes of "running," she could sense her body shutting down. Donna collapsed not quite in the woods but on the outskirts near a cold dirt road looking up at the heavens. Thinking about the house that God helped her find and how fortunate she was to be outside of it.

◆ ◆ ◆

Sheriff Marvin stood outside the chilly emergency room peering in at Donna, her body almost completely covered in bandages. A nurse finished adjusting her blankets then exited the room and approached him.

"No change since you spoke with her yesterday. She hasn't said anything different. She still keeps rambling about that tall man with the mustache."

"Okay, I think the boyfriend will be here shortly. Maybe I'll try again tomorrow once she's got a little more rest. In the meantime, I'll see what he has to say," Sheriff Marvin responded.

"Sounds good to me, Sheriff. I'll keep you posted."

"Thanks, Leann."

As the nurse walked off down the corridor, Donna's ex-boyfriend, Roy, approached. He powerwalked up to the Sheriff who was still lingering outside the doors of Donna's room.

"Oh, my God. Wh—What happened to her?! Why is she covered in bandages, Deputy?" Roy cried, becoming visibly emotional.

"It's Sheriff. Sheriff Marvin. I take it you're Roy McCanty, the boyfriend?"

"Yes, sir, we spoke on the phone yesterday. Why didn't you tell me about her condition?!"

"Listen, Roy, I need you to calm down. She needs to rest. We can't have you out here shouting and waking her up. I didn't tell you yesterday because you wouldn't be able to get here until today with the storm and all. No sense in me causing you a bunch of worry if you can't do anything about it. And I certainly didn't want you acting all crazy, like you're starting to right now, and driving in that cluster fuck outside."

"What happened to her?" Roy said, sobbing.

"Well, that's why I need to talk to you. You see, this

whole thing just don't make no sense. You told me on the phone that you all got in a bit of a tiff the day we found her and that she just stormed off heading for her momma's house."

"That's right. She left because she found some rubbers in my jacket. I wasn't cheating on her though! I shouldn't have let her go. Jesus, this is all my fault."

"RELAX. Listen, Roy, if you wanna help Donna, you need to stay calm and give me the information we need to figure this out."

"Okay, okay. I'm good. I'm gonna hold it together."

"Appreciate that, I know it's difficult. She didn't get but a few miles from your house when her truck broke down and she said that she tried to walk. I figure she was motivated by what happened to old Tom Kelp a few days ago. After about a mile or so, she says she ended up on Solomon Road hoping to find a house in the woods to warm up at."

"Solomon Road? Where's that?"

"You sure you don't know what she's talking about, Roy?"

"I never heard of no Solomon Road."

"Well, you never heard of it because it don't exist. Nonetheless, she claims she was there praying and that God led her to a house. It just gets weirder from there."

"Tell me what she said, Sheriff."

"She says a large man with a mustache lived in the house. That he was keepin' girls in the basement. Said he cut them up with a big old pair scissors. He liked to 'cut the black parts offa them' whatever the fuck that means. Lastly, she claims she got away when one of them attacked him."

"What? Oh God, what are you saying, h—he fucking dismembered her?"

"No, Roy, no. There was no man, no house, no Solomon Road. At least we don't think so, but it's hard to be certain. However, she did suffer from severe deep frostbite which is most likely what caused the affected extremities to fall off."

"But she's missing body parts?"

"Unfortunately, yes, Roy. I don't know if she went down another road and got confused about the street name and we have a psychopath with dismembered girls in his basement on our hands, or if this could all be explained as a result of the storm. This weather don't make it no easier to investigate. My hope is that this is some sick delusion, derived from her shock and trauma but that's where I need you to help me, Roy. I need you to tell me if she's ever talked like this before."

Roy tried to hold back the tears from streaming full force. He bit down on his lip and straightened up.

"About four years ago, Donna started hearing voices. People in her head telling her to do things. She said she thought they were nuns from the Catholic school she used to go to. At the time, it wasn't uncommon for her to say she seen things and become paranoid. She was diagnosed as schizophrenic but she's been medicated ever since. Nothing like that ever happened again. It was only for about a period of three months. I thought she was cured…"

Sheriff Marvin looked Roy square in his glossy eyes. "And when exactly is the last time she took her medication?"

MORE THAN
A FEELING

Aunt Mary was always my favorite, all my fondest childhood memories seem to include her. I'm sure tons of other cool things happened when I was a kid, my mom and dad were great people. They created the kind of environment in our household that never permitted a bad night. No arguments or deception, just all the feel-good wholesomeness that you'd expect growing up in a friendly suburban neighborhood in the late 70s.

We were quite well-off and mom and dad had no qualms about spoiling me. In part, possibly because I was never a brat about it. At a young age, I was still mature enough to understand that it was somewhat abnormal to get the sort of gifts and visit the extravagant places we traveled to. I knew I was fortunate but never acted as if I should be entitled to anything. I was always grateful and, at times, even felt a little guilty about it in comparison to some of my other friends.

Considering our family's stability and the unique opportunities that always seemed to be within grasp throughout my adolescence, it's a tad peculiar that the only memories I can seem to salvage from that period are of my Aunt Mary.

We connected on so many levels, our interests in all things strange and unexplainable were something that my parents didn't necessarily disapprove of, just more like something they didn't relate to. They could surround me with the newest toys and clothes, which, again, I was always thankful for, but I was never as attentive as when Aunt Mary arrived.

She was an odd duck, like a magician often appearing without forewarning. Sometimes I might arrive home from school to find her in the parlor reading a book, while gently pulling on a Pall Mall from her drawn-out cigarette holder.

Even the way she smoked was thrilling to me. I enjoyed watching her French inhale and blow tiny smoke rings toward the ceiling. She liked to wear a variety of interesting hats that were showy and served to shroud her features, further adding to her mysteriousness. She dressed sharply but always donned patterns that were unique, fashion firsts, at least compared to what my parents and other adults around us wore.

She gave me books about disturbing hauntings, ghost stories and spirits getting caught between the afterlife and heaven. She told me about miraculous events she'd heard of from other like-minded people or researched herself.

My mom was actually pretty upset when my Aunt Mary and I had our first discussion about death. I was only five years old and had never brought up the subject before, but it was like she knew we had this connection.

She could tell I was like her before I had even begun to form opinions on the world around me or my true interests. My mom was concerned that introducing a concept like death could create phobias or keep me up late at night, contemplating when my own end might be or how it might come about.

These morbid curiosities did, in reality, overrun my mind, but not in the manner my mother suggested. I never feared death. My Aunt Mary posed these things to me in such a way that we examined them together and often debated the possible outcomes.

Between us, death did not seem like something to dread but more like an adventure, the utmost unknown in humanity that we would one day become privy to. What a treat it would be to finally know, and until then, we would debate reincarnation, heaven, hell, and everything in between.

It was just after my seventh birthday when my parents hosted a party at our house that would see a variety of people from our neighborhood break bread together and share in local gossip. I didn't care much for these gatherings because they always separated the kids from the adults.

We would all be told to stay in the den and play with each other while the adults remained in the parlor, chatting over a drink. Which meant it was one of the only times that Aunt Mary was at our house and I couldn't be around her.

It felt like torture. I would sit almost outside of the play area and try to listen carefully, waiting patiently to hear what topics Aunt Mary might uncork. Many of the other neighborhood children were enamored with the selection of toys and games we had but I couldn't have been more disinterested.

After allowing the adults to settle in, I was able to peer around the door frame and get a vantage point that let me see most of them. Thankfully, Aunt Mary chose a seat in my line of sight, most likely because it had an inviting maple-colored standing ashtray within arm's length.

No one else in the room stood out to me until my Aunt Mary snubbed out her Pall Mall and started a spooky sort of old parlor game that I'd seen her do only once before. The game consisted of her asking different party-goers for an item they possessed—any item of their choice.

Then she would touch the article they chose for a moment and tell the owner something only they would know about it (where it was purchased, what they used it for, et cetera). But the eeriest part of the whole charade was that she was always right. Which meant it wasn't really a charade, I suppose.

The befuddlement and confusion on the people's faces said it all, they were now believers. Even if they'd wanted to paint her as a kook out of jealousy over her gift, they were always too stunned to pull it off, their expressions told all.

It was probably my favorite thing that I'd ever seen in my whole life, and therefore, I was completely overcome with excitement. I had to pee really badly but there was no way I could miss this. I pinched my legs together and exposed my childish grin, it outweighed any displeasure I felt.

She began by approaching Mrs. Bartel, slowly inching toward her with a sweet but mischievous spirit about her. She lived at the end of the street and had always seemed like a quiet, kind woman. It was hard to tell for sure because she usually kept to herself but my guess was this woman hadn't a bad bone in her body.

She never had children to my knowledge and her husband, Marty, I would eventually learn, passed away a few years before I was born. She removed a small white handkerchief from her purse and handed it to Aunt Mary. She held on a bit tighter than you'd expect when relinquishing an item to someone. It was almost as if she didn't want to let go.

"I hope this is clean," Aunt Mary joked with a smile, stealing a laugh from the crowd and Mrs. Bartel.

She concentrated a bit and looked down at her, becoming a little more serious.

"Marty is glad you still have this. It makes him feel warm inside knowing you still think about him."

Mrs. Bartel held back her tears, a mix of sadness and joy clearly compelling her. She took back the handkerchief and thanked her kindly. Then, what seemed like a look of comfort came over her.

She eyed her next subject and moved toward the dapper clean-cut Mr. Billings who sat beside the fireplace confidently, legs crossed. I'm not sure who invited Mr. Billings to the party as he was not from our neighborhood, nor a friend of the family. However, this friend of a friend seemed rather charming.

I'd noticed earlier that Aunt Mary seemed to strike up a long conversation with him. It felt like she was showing more interest in him than she tended to show any other man. Maybe she had some sort of crush on him. Whatever the case, it was out of the ordinary and, at least to me, quite noticeable.

She beckoned him using a gesture that suggested he choose an article for her to feel. She smiled with him; face painted with a thin blush. He seemed unamused by the game but not aggravated.

"No, I think I will have to pass on this one, Mary. I can't think of anything to give you."

"Oh, c'mon, Tom, don't be silly, just give her anything," the always intrusive Mr. Hines butted in, standing by the coatrack across from the two.

"I'm afraid I don't have anything," he reiterated.

Mr. Hines then grabbed a black leather glove (that I could only assume was Mr. Billings's) that hung out of one of the coat pockets.

"Just use this." He tossed it at Aunt Mary.

Mr. Billings didn't object but studied Aunt Mary carefully as the glove contacted her flesh. Suddenly, Aunt Mary twitched as if she was briefly electrocuted. She dropped the glove on the ground, eyes wide and bulging.

My Aunt's typical "in control of the conversation" attitude had vanished. She turned away from Mr. Billings quickly and looked at the group, who were now concerned but even more curious.

"I'm sorry, I'm—I'm not feeling very well. I need to step away for a bit," Aunt Mary explained.

She never picked up the glove, she just exited the parlor and headed for the kitchen. My mother, clearly concerned for her sister, quickly followed behind her.

I could hear them in the kitchen when she asked her if she was okay and to explain what the scene in the parlor was all about. Aunt Mary didn't really broadcast what had happened, at least not in front of me. She just reiterated that she was feeling a bit under the weather suddenly and asked if it would be okay if she spent some time with me, away from the party.

She stayed in the playroom with us kids for the rest of the evening. I tried with every shred of my, at that time, minimal intellectuality, to reason with her and get her to share with me what the hell had just happened. To divulge what dimension of Mr. Billings she had seen that alarmed her so much, but she wouldn't.

She did tell me I would understand someday but that day couldn't be today. Of course, it would be her to say something of that nature, giving me another mystery to obsess about.

However, this was very unlike my Aunt Mary. This was the first and only question I ever asked her that she did not give me a completely transparent answer to.

Two days later, my mom came into my bedroom crying hysterically. I was immediately injected with a horrible feeling. I'd never seen my mother cry before and I just knew it was about Aunt Mary.

Although my mom wouldn't tell me the whole story that day, she did tell me that Aunt Mary passed away. I was crushed. My hero and one of a kind spiritual companion had been stolen from me. Receiving that gut-wrenching news was undoubtedly the worst part of my entire life.

For a long time, I was angry but I didn't know who to be angry with, so I just buried it. I swallowed the permanently bitter pill and felt it stewing deep inside me without tire. I did my best not to take it out on others. I know Aunt Mary would not have wanted that.

She would have wanted me to be a decent, respectable young man and share the mindset template we'd shaped together with others. She'd want me to continue to find a way to humbly drive the discussions we'd had about our approach to life and death.

I never forgot about my Aunt Mary, but as I grew older, I avoided talking about her as a way to cope with my grief and anger. It was a debilitating concoction of emotions for my preteen psyche to absorb.

There were entire summers that I recall spending in bed, my friends at my window on their Huffy bikes, pleading for me to come outside but I just couldn't. I had my own thoughts on the sad subject constantly circulating. The only thing I truly knew was that everyone didn't want me to know how she died, but it wasn't something they could stop me from finding out.

In my heart, there was no doubt it had something to do with Mr. Billings. She was so disturbed by her encounter with him on that unusual night, that much was obvious to me. What did she see that evening?

I constantly presented my theories to my mother in an effort to get her to confirm or disregard my suspicions. As usual, she remained mum on the topic, neither agreeing nor denying, instead just repeating the same cryptic set of words that my Aunt Mary left me with, "You will understand someday."

I still thought about her every night and as I became old enough to walk places by myself, I made it a point to visit her regularly. I left a fresh set of flowers on her grave at the end of every month and made sure the site remained well-kept.

I would sit for a while, no matter how cold or hot it was outside, no matter who I was supposed to hang out with that day or if I had a date with a girl. Everything stopped at the end of the month at Northgate Cemetery. She was the sole person that I truly cared to remain popular with.

I'd spend the first few moments telling her how much I loved her and missed her. Recalling all the wacky times we shared together and things that were happening in my life now that I wanted to keep her updated on.

I must have looked really weird to others visiting their loved ones somberly as I laughed while conversing with her tombstone. Aunt Mary was different though, they could never understand that we weren't afraid to die, we looked forward to it.

For each question I asked her and the current events I shared with her, I always received a response. Almost like her voice was in my head answering and commenting. I don't know if it was just my own subconscious filling in each of the blanks the way I remembered that she would talk to me or not.

Maybe it was my own way of coping with the grief of losing the person I related to the most in life, or maybe, just maybe, she was finding a way to communicate with me. I did find it strange that the only question I asked her that I didn't get an answer to was around the last day I saw her.

"When will I understand? You said I would understand someday. I need to know what happened to you."

I had to wait until my 16th birthday to know the entire truth of the matter—a little over nine years after her death. My mom sat me down with some old yellowed newspaper clippings in hand and a low-spirited look about her.

She explained that on the night of the party, Aunt Mary had a passionate conversation with her once everyone had dispersed. She said earlier in the evening Aunt Mary had been chatting with Mr. Billings and taken a real shine to him. They'd talked about maybe getting together for a date sometime after the party and shared some details about what their interests were, where they worked, lived, et cetera.

As she continued to expound, Mom claimed that everything changed when his glove contacted her hand. She described seeing a blinding light and a cold darkness beyond it. And within that darkness, she saw that very same glove wrapped tightly around the throat of a young boy, close to my age at the time.

The vision rattled her profoundly but she did her best to not display that. She didn't want to let on her newfound awareness, better Mr. Billings saw the game as a harmless charade than for him to consider that she knew a more sinister truth.

She was certain that he was hurting children, and immediately, her first instinct was to protect me. That's why she left the room and stayed beside me and the rest of the children until the evening concluded. When she told my mom, at first, she didn't know what to think, it seemed crazy to her to believe everything just based on Aunt Mary feeling his glove.

She told my mom never to let him in the house or near me again, and if she disobeyed her request, then she would never speak to her again. She wanted to go to the police immediately and report a complaint but she understood that the validity of her vision would probably be criticized.

Mom then explained that my father entered the discussion and found the whole argument to be quite far-fetched and wanted Aunt Mary to sleep on it before filing a complaint. Mr. Billings was a friend of a friend's and he thought it might be in bad taste to accuse someone based on the "vision" alone.

Aunt Mary disagreed and asked for a sheet of paper and a pen just prior to leaving. When she got into her car, she wrote out everything she experienced that night, down to the finest detail. She set the note in an envelope and placed it inside her glove box.

The next morning, neighbors found Aunt Mary's body in her car. She'd just finished parking in the driveway of her house when someone apparently blindsided her and proceeded to strangle her to death. When the police searched the car, they found the note she'd left detailing her suspicions about Mr. Billings. It didn't take them long to make their way to his house and execute a search.

They tore the place apart and, after breaking through an old wall in the basement, they found two young boys inside. One had been strangled, his larynx crushed to a pulp by a much larger hand, just as Aunt Mary had described in her metaphysical vision.

The boy was found buried under the dirt floor of the basement in a makeshift wooden casket that bore his initials. The second was found alive in a cage with a water and food bowl like you'd have for an animal. Apparently, Billings viewed these kids as his pets and once he played too rough with the first one, he'd found himself another.

They'd each been kidnapped from different towns that were not too far from our own neighborhood. In the end, she'd given her own life to save that boy and to protect me from a monster.

When my mom finally broke it all down for me, she probably thought I was old enough to handle some of the more gruesome details and maybe hoped it would provide me a bit of closure. She wanted to help answer some questions that I'd never stopped asking but closure was never something I'd sought. I didn't want anything about Aunt Mary to be final, she would always live on forever in my heart and maybe in other ways besides that too.

A few days later, the end of the month was upon us once again. I found myself in front of her plot on our favorite holiday, October 31st, Halloween. This time, I was looking down at her with a newfound respect, as if it was even possible to think she was cooler than I already did.

Trick or treating together was one of the best memories I had with her, so of course, I dressed up. I went to about eight thrift stores trying to find the same old glow-in-the-dark matching skeleton outfits that we'd worn the last year she took me out. Except I'd done some growing since then. This time, I would need two adult size costumes.

After days of searching, I'd found a spookily similar outfit, damn near identical to the ones we'd had. The only difference with these costumes was that the bones were an orange color instead of neon yellow. I suppose it didn't matter; real bones were neither of those colors anyway.

It was just getting dark when I got to her grave. I took out the second costume and laid it out over her stone and began to sob. There was a new weight as to why Aunt Mary was here now. I wasn't expecting to get emotional but I couldn't hold it back.

"Hey, what are you putting on her grave!?" a voice yelled from behind me.

I suppose it did look a bit odd. I was dressed in full skeleton garb putting a costume over a headstone. I thought it might be the groundskeeper at first but the voice sounded too juvenile.

I turned around to see a young man of similar height and age standing a few yards back. He seemed awfully protective of the grave, like he knew her intimately. It struck me as odd since I didn't have any cousins or family that age besides myself that would really have known her.

"This is my Aunt Mary's grave. I usually come here on Halloween to see her. I know it probably seems really weird but she used to take me out as a kid. This is how I deal with missing her," I explained.

The boy looked mystified. His eyelids pulled apart while his jaw sat slightly agape.

"Are you okay, man?" I asked him, growing a little concerned over his intensity.

"Your Aunt Mary, she saved my life. She told the police where I was. Without her, I might still be in that basement tonight," he said with tears welling up in both eyes.

"Oh, my God, it's you!" I finally spat out, astonished. I was nearly speechless.

"I've been coming by here every once in a while to see her, I know some of the stupider people do things to graves on Halloween but I wanted to make sure nothing happened to your Aunt's."

"Thank you, that's very kind of you to protect her. My Aunt was the best. She was the nicest person you could have hoped to ever meet. She's my best friend, that's why I still come here," I said, breaking down along with him.

"I love your Aunt so much. I think about her every day. I just wish there was some way I could repay her. I just can't shake this feeling sometimes that I'm responsible. If I didn't get in that car with Billings, she might still be alive."

"It's not your fault, you can't think like that. Do you want to know something about my Aunt Mary?"

The boy nodded his head, wiping the thick streams of tears away again.

"All we talked about is what happens in the next life. She believed in a lot of things and couldn't wait to find out what came after all this," I said, pointing around us. "She wouldn't want you feeling that way."

"Thanks, man. Okay, I'm sorry I disturbed you while you were visiting your Aunt. I just wanted to make sure she was okay."

The boy turned away, heading back toward the gates that he entered from. After he took a few steps, I heard that same voice in my head when I usually talked to Aunt Mary. She didn't want him to go. I ran down towards him and hollered out.

"Hey, wait a minute! What's your name?"

The boy turned around and looked back at me, still overwhelmed with emotion.

"Derek," he replied.

"Do you wanna go trick or treating with me, Derek?" I asked him.

"I would but I, I don't have a costume and, well, don't you wanna be with your Aunt right now?"

On that calm autumn night, immediately after those words left his mouth, a gust of wind picked up out of nowhere. A chilly air near Aunt Mary's grave blew the second costume I'd laid out for her right towards us and practically left the fabric draped over Derek.

"I think she wants us to go together," I explained.

Derek smiled and wiped the tears from his eyes for what I hoped would be the last time. We both said goodbye and told Aunt Mary we loved her. Then he donned her glowing skeleton suit and we headed for the gates together.

THIS PERSON DOES EXIST

Being sick sucks, however, that's not to say it's completely without benefits. Martin's anxiety was fairly mild, bordering on non-existent but still had the occasional flare-up. He didn't feel guilty embellishing it to take a few days off from work here and there.

Being tight on cash was cool with him since he didn't harbor a single outgoing bone in his entire body. He'd much rather play video games, chat with friends online, or fall down the proverbial internet wormhole.

He witnessed many other co-workers abuse the rash of alleged "anxiety issues" that everyone in society seemed to be stricken with these days in a much more egregious manner. There was one girl in particular who was absent more of the year than she was there. It was so blatant that people at work had branded her "Call-out Kelly," which made Martin chuckle each time he heard it.

In his humble opinion, he wasn't doing anything that disrespectful. What was the problem with taking a day or two to order pizza (his favorite edible pastime) and read the latest gossip on the cyber message boards?

The Family and Medical Leave Act had been put forth back in '93 to give people an out from work without any negative retaliation if they were having family, medical, or mental issues. The mental issues portion was where people seemed to be able to manipulate. Most doctors aren't psychologists and, even if they were, there was plenty of wiggle room.

It was pretty much as simple as researching and noting the symptoms of an anxiety disorder and then putting on a mildly credible performance. Almost anyone could pull it off. And if your own doctor was suspicious or didn't want to sign you off, you needn't look far to find one that would.

They were already salivating at the thought of tossing another unnecessary prescription to fatten their own pocket, always at the self-justified expense of creating another societal zombie. About five minutes of online research could locate one of these conscienceless consultants.

Martin didn't have to enlist that much effort. His longtime practitioner, Dr. Earl Wigman, found his diagnosis more than plausible. It was almost a bit concerning how quickly he jumped on board with the concept, like he'd seen it stirring inside him for quite some time. To Martin, he was just gassing him up, but to Dr. Wigman, this was a long-overdue step.

What did Wigman really know though? He saw him about once a year, maybe twice if he got the flu or something. He was certainly no shrink, during most examinations it felt like he barely paid attention and just went through the motions.

Sure, Martin knew he was a little weird and probably more anti-social than the average Joe, but this wasn't something that was detrimental in his eyes. It's not like he was depressed every day, he just envisioned human existence through a more futuristic lens.

He understood his preference for virtual relationships made him different. By thirty-four, most men would have a sense of urgency, wanting to figure out who to spend the rest of their days beside. Martin believed that he could find a greater satisfaction being left to his own devices. If he was fine with this ideology, why couldn't others be?

Having his freedom, his individuality, overrode any exhilaration dwelling within him regarding potential in the flesh romances. The same philosophy applied to friendships. His preference was to be available by his own watch.

If he didn't crave conversation, he could simply appear offline instead of the additional chore of having to explain in person or by phone. Life was simplified for him that way since he'd never been particularly savvy with spoken words.

It didn't help that he looked like a weirdo either. He had curly black hair that was impossible to style. Whichever way he parted it and regardless of how much product he put into it, his hair looked like complete shit.

In addition to that permanent annoyance, he had one of those embarrassing short beards that was only able to grow patches in certain areas. Whenever he did attempt to let it accumulate, the end result would always seem like he'd glued a few clumps of recently trimmed pubes to his face.

His appearance issues and self-appointed isolation were most likely the reasons he'd been attracted to factory work. The communal interaction was minimal.

If he avoided any fuck-ups (which was easy enough, this was a factory, not a space station) he could almost completely evade any conversation. Plus, with Wigman's diagnosis, he could control and schedule his moments of reprieve.

It didn't really hurt anyone, he reasoned. The worst of the quiet damages would be felt by his employer. They would usually need additional laborers to account for the workload he and the others that decided to play the system left behind. So, if you thought about it, in a way he was helping his co-workers score some overtime.

He was forcing the factory to reach deeper into their pockets but this corporation was worth tens of millions—a "cry me a river" kind of situation if there ever was one. If it was a mom and pop joint, he might have examined the moral matters more closely.

He could see management was far from thrilled when he brought in Wigman's note but there was little they could do as he was otherwise an admirable worker. Avoiding a lawsuit is any sensible corporation's top priority. If he didn't abuse it excessively, he wouldn't be ruffling the feathers of anyone that mattered.

Now, for the next few days, it was time to play. Martin was planning to start his Monday off on the message boards. Even though he'd been on them most of last night, there were constantly new topics to review and updates to current subjects that were already on his radar.

Often times, the most recent whispers required further investigation. Many of the discussions were of a conspiratorial nature, which meant there was plenty of both mis and disinformation to evaluate. It never took him long to find something that piqued his interest and today was no exception.

He quickly found himself deep down the rabbit hole clicking from one absurd concept to the next. It was a fun game, alluring, considering you never know where you might end up. The mystery of it all was highly arousing to him, especially when he reached a really strange one. Those were the ones he lived for, the unexplainable, the bizarre, the mysterious.

He first sifted through an assortment of overly paranoid posts. The first of which aimed at painting a progressively more disturbing portrait regarding the future of Artificial Intelligence. It began quite cartoonish with tales of technologies being implanted in people, by guardians that were only described as "The Controllers." It was followed by the more feasible but constantly regurgitated sort of prophecy that Terminator 2 gave way to. Robots prepping for war with society, a takeover imminent based on our own human ignorance.

A few clicks deeper and he'd moved back to machines meshing with man, becoming one by technology infusion. Some source links were embedded, providing test cases of engineers who had already fused microchips into the human brain, granting people abilities that were anything but God-given. Increasing intelligence, restoring senses, and giving back movement to previously lame limbs were some examples offered.

These were things he'd seen before and found highly engrossing, but not today. He'd already amassed a deep familiarity with those topics, the hunger for something different lingered inside him. It didn't take him long to find it, the internet's most recent gift lay at the bottom of his flickering monitor.

The post was titled "This Person Does Not Exist." Martin thought this peculiar, the exact sort of thing that raised his antenna. A post with little explanation, something he would have to dig into and figure out for himself. The few lines of minuscule information available read as follows:

"Strange New Website Uses AI to Conjure Faces of People That Aren't Real. It seems to only create a picture of each person from the neck up, but it can be men, women, or children of all shapes and colors from what I've noticed so far. Also, sometimes accessories will randomly appear with the person such as glasses, hats, and jewelry.

Look at the teeth and ears, that is where the disfigurement can occasionally be noticed. I'm not sure why exactly but they have been appearing with regularity. It's possible that the detail required in those specific regions may be more complex for the AI to produce.

Refreshing your screen will create a new person each time.

I've also noticed some bizarre imperfections that are harder to describe. They look like something you'd see in a NASA deep space photo, almost like black holes are sitting on or inside of their skin… garbled clusters of flesh also appear on or beside them during certain generations.

This is most likely due to a gremlin in the technology. It's safe to assume this is a low dollar funded project being that there seem to be zero traces of it anywhere. Defects aside, it's all still very entrancing. They have this realistic, creepy sort of quality to them. I can't seem to stop wanting to generate new ones, I keep wondering what the next one will look like. Will it be nearly flawless or another strange (unintentional?) horror…

When I locate an image that I truly find captivating, I will usually download the picture since refreshing deletes the prior person spawned. I've run these through multiple sophisticated facial recognition databases and also reached out to other web sleuths with notable credentials. No one has been able to find a trace of these people. It's seeming more and more like the website's title isn't false advertising, these people do not exist. I can't help but wonder if they don't exist, what is their purpose?

Does anyone have knowledge relating to the creator(s) of this site and what its motive might be? There seems to be no public information on this evasive topic. The site just exists but apparently the people don't…"

At the bottom of the strange posting, the author "TechnicalTeddy24" had provided a link to the site in question. There were no comments on the post at the time, probably because it was put up only about an hour ago.

He would be the first to get a crack at it. Martin knew he should probably begin with research before even looking at the site, but his curiosity was getting the better of him. Black holes and garbled flesh were too bizarre, too appealing for him to control himself.

He clicked the link and up came the site, displaying nothing more than a single digital picture from the neck up. The first one to display was a portrait of an older man. His hair more salt than pepper, his eyebrows dark and bushy, sitting above a pair of silver wire-framed glasses.

He was slightly wrinkled but had a healthy olive complexion. Nothing really out of the ordinary about this one. The background was blurred but not in an unusual manner. Everything about him looked pretty legitimate. The man could have been someone he casually passed on the subway on any normal day when he was en route to work.

He then remembered the post's explicit suggestion, asking readers to examine the ears and teeth closely. Martin noticed the way the old man's head was positioned only left one ear visible but nothing looked out of place. He then magnified the old man's teeth, which from his current vantage point looked quite normal.

Once the image was blown up, it was easy to see the new revelation, the teeth on the bottom were distinguished singularly by black lines separating them, however, the top row displayed like five of his teeth were one. It was like the man had a lone, solid bar of enamel running across the top of his gum line. This was very abnormal indeed.

He didn't really know what to think of this exposure. So far, the notes of the initial post seemed to be accurate. Sometimes people have a tendency to jump to conclusions on message boards and promote unsubstantiated claims without an objective investigative routine. So far, however, it seemed as if the article was being conservative with its deductions, thus adding to its credibility.

He decided he must generate another and see if it could be replicated or if something different would arise. The second person to face him was an Asian woman, her eyes directed toward the camera lens, burrowing back through him.

She had straight black hair that was tied back by a bright red headscarf that matched the collar of her shirt. Her lips were closed so he would not be able to inspect her teeth, but he made note they were painted with a pink, sparkly cosmetic product.

In addition, he'd noticed her ears seemed suspicious. The left one was pierced with a round silver ball attached to it but looked normal even upon magnifying. The right ear, however, displayed traits of what the message board reported.

It was this sort of knotted ball of meat dangling from the side of her face. When zooming in to the maximum, it looked more psychedelic, like the vibrant innards of a kaleidoscope melting inside an oil spill. Something told him to save it. This one disturbed him for reasons that were not immediately clear to him.

He refreshed again to reveal a much more upsetting photo. This one looked to be a white male, his arms and general build made him seem like he might be in his late 20s. The face was harder to peg. The man's eyes were glued shut and his short dark hair was arranged in a spiked, bed-head fashion. His nose appeared to be liquifying right off of his face. It oozed downward, falling toward what was, by far, the most concerning area to show itself yet.

A gaping vortex sat swirling where his chin and throat would normally be. More of the vivid colorful madness that he'd seen in the close-up of the prior photo was displayed, in addition to the "black hole" previously mentioned in the post. Everything else about the man looked so real which made the impossible parts so much more difficult to digest.

He would save this one as well in an effort to have a record of the different anomalies that he was observing on the site. He spent the next couple of hours reaching out to fellow researchers in his community. Martin was providing them the links via email and attaching the strange images in question, while still in the middle of his own research.

Typically, after a few hours of research, he would find a few bones to chew on. At least a tidbit of information that might spark something, more evidence forthcoming with each additional hour he committed. That was not the case today.

Four hours later, he was equally as perplexed as the article's author, which is a feeling that had rarely resided inside him. He'd never encountered a topic that he could find absolutely no trace of. There were not even any other similar posts inquiring about the site. It felt like he'd stumbled onto some great unknown, an outlandish secret. At least for now anyway.

Research can create a large appetite, especially unsuccessful research. Martin had already become impatient, feeling he should have found a clue long ago. He decided he would run down a few blocks and grab some beef fried rice and chicken fingers from Lucky Star.

It was his Chinese restaurant of choice and also the most convenient of take-out spots within his vicinity. He picked up the phone and called in his order, then quickly snagged his coat and headed for the door.

Lucky Star was awesome, just the thought of the fatty delights had him salivating. Since he was unable to receive any quick gratification mentally, he would have to seek it with his taste buds. Fucking weird-ass site, it was really gnawing at him, he needed to know the rationale. He would eventually, after his pick-me-up, the grub would serve as a recharge for him.

Martin really wasn't bothered so much by walking through a sea of people, as long as they didn't interact with him. Stay modest and move on had become his motto.

He always found himself apologizing and moving forward whenever a bum or drug addict approached him with a question. New York was overflowing with them; it was ironic how much he tried to avoid human interaction yet he'd chosen to live in a city with more people than just about anywhere.

Martin was well aware he didn't have the capacity to recall every person he saw or record every stranger he encountered. Thousands and thousands of people's faces, captured momentarily before being purged from his memories altogether due to their lack of personal relevance. Today would be the day that logic changed for him, at least for one face, for the most part a very beautiful one. The only problem was, it wasn't supposed to exist.

He couldn't believe his eyes when they came upon her. It was the Asian woman from his downloaded picture, the lone standstill in a mass of bustling bodies. He believed it to be her for a handful of reasons:

1. She was only about 20 yards away from him and his view of her wasn't obstructed

2. Her red headscarf and matching collar popped out from everyone else

3. A closed mouth painted with pink lipstick sparkled in the afternoon sunlight

4. Her head was turned slightly so he could only see her left ear but that was the ear that bore the same silver ball earring from the picture

He unlocked his phone and reviewed the photo to make sure his eyes weren't deceiving him. No doubt about it, that was the woman. What made the situation even more hair-raising was that she was staring a hole right through him. Out of a crowd of hundreds, they were the only two not moving. They were the only two just staring at each other.

Martin had no idea what to do next. Should he just head to Lucky Star and hope to lose her in the crowd?

A more curious, risky part of him wanted to approach the girl, but then again, things like this don't just happen. In reality, there had to be a more sinister reason for an impossibility of this nature materializing, the gremlin had found its way out of the matrix.

Before he could decide what action to take, the woman smiled at him. From his vantage point, he couldn't tell for certain, but it looked like her mouth might contain the same kind of barred enamel that he'd seen in the first photo of the old man. A chill ran down his spine, generating a body jerking twitch. The woman turned her head slightly, revealing a ball of knotted flesh in place of where her ear should've resided.

He angled his phone up and snapped a few quick pictures of the woman from a distance before turning around and heading back to his apartment. He didn't feel safe anymore, something was off about the woman and he didn't want to find out what.

He needed to lose her but decided he should use a different route back to avoid tipping her off to his living quarters. Somehow, she knew what city he lived in already. He wasn't sure if it would make a difference, but to him, the precaution was logical. At the very least, he prayed it would buy him a little more time before she reached him.

He rushed through the crowd of equally pushy New Yorkers, knocking people aside in a way he had never previously. A fear of the unknown raced about his body as his heart pounded.

His sweat streamed down from his brow while the brisk temperature shot him with a chilly feeling. After a lapse in time, it was hard to tell how much, he looked back and the woman was gone. Upon registering that he'd shook her, he blazed the trail of the fastest route back to his studio.

Once in his building, he took the stairs in exchange for the elevator, rushing to the seventh floor. He quickly burst inside, dead bolting the door and setting the chain lock. He was breathing heavily, still unsure of what exactly was going on. He paced the living room before finally sinking into the couch, not any less disturbed than before.

He put forth an effort to calm himself, stiffening his body in an attempt to suppress his trembles. He needed to slow the racing thoughts enough to be able to think. He was an intelligent guy, he could figure out a more rational explanation. His wheels began to turn finally, forcing him into a less emotional poise.

In his mind, he began going through possible scenarios but none of them made any sense. They all seemed to point to one of three possibilities:

1. He had mistakenly identified the woman, even though he was only a short distance away, somehow, his eyes had deceived him

2. A woman invented by AI moments ago crossed over from the digital realm into the plane of human existence

3. He was having a severe mental breakdown

Updates? Comments? His thoughts were getting him nowhere fast, he needed to check the post again. The best he could hope for was that someone had updated it with additional findings. He wasn't confident since he hadn't found anything himself but it was still the most sensible next step.

He hammered down his desktop passcode onto the keys and navigated back to the message board. He clicked the post and refreshed the page just to be sure the most updated information was reflected. And there it was, the key to erasing the slew of uncertainties that were pounding on his brain. The comment indicator had changed from zero to one, which, in turn, birthed a nervousness and sense of anticipation grinding about in his guts.

The comment was from the same individual that had put up the original post, "TechnicalTeddy24" and had just been updated about ten minutes ago. Holding his breath, he clicked the comment and began to read it to himself.

"DO NOT DOWNLOAD THE IMAGES!

I downloaded three of these images to run through the facial recognition search engines I mentioned in my initial post. I know people post fabrications in this forum frequently and readers will probably not believe what I'm about to write, but I beg you to heed my warning. It sounds so outlandish… I wouldn't believe it if I hadn't seen it with my own eyes.

THE PEOPLE EXIST. Somehow, they found me, they've been following me and I have no idea why.

I'm terrified but I've figured out that it has something to do with downloading the images. I can say that with measured reason because the three I downloaded are the ones that have appeared. The others, which I only viewed, I am yet to see, it's too specific to be a coincidence.

I don't know what they want but each encounter is becoming more threatening. At first, I thought I'd been drugged, I felt loony. I quickly realized this wasn't the case when I saw the second one. Sure, maybe the first one was a fluke, someone that looked like one of the pictures, my research could have just oversaturated my brain. But once I saw the second, I knew something extraordinary was afoot. He followed me on the subway, stalking me with an ominous approach. His dripping eyes stared a hole through me from the end of the train. I couldn't understand why the others around me weren't reacting to him.

I managed to evade him for long enough to exit the train but he was still in pursuit. A fraction of my anxiety was transposed with relief when I saw an officer. I ran up to the cop and pointed the man out who was still in slow stride in my direction but clearly visible as there was no crowd currently on the tier.

The officer asked if I was alright. When I ignored his question and again asked him to confront the man, he informed me there was no one on the tier. I asked him to look again, this time pointing right at him. He couldn't have been more than ten feet away at this point. He kindly obliged me looking in the exact area I'd directed him but it made no difference. He gave me the same response, now looking at me like a complete crackpot.

NO ONE ELSE CAN SEE THEM.

I couldn't talk to him much longer; the man was closing in on me. I ran up the concrete steps, exiting the subdivision and luckily was able to hail a cab before he surfaced. I was dropped off at my workplace only to be greeted by the third one. She was by far the most terrifying, her head wholly distorted into a dead pool of revolving static pigments. The cycle felt almost hypnotic, it took great effort and concentration for me to pull my gaze off of her, but thankfully, I was able to.

I ran upstairs and locked myself in the men's room without the static being seeing me, I have no idea what it might do if it gets a hold of me. I'm posting this so there is a record and, hopefully, others don't make the same mistake I did.

My name is Donald Parsons and my current residence is 75 Woodmont Ave Chicago IL. I never believed in God but may God help me."

A new form of fear dawned on Martin. Sinister illustrations of what these entities' possible motives might be surged inside him. "No one else can see them," he thought, reaching for his cell phone. He opened the pictures he'd taken earlier of the strange Asian woman, except now it was only a picture of a crowd. She'd somehow vanished. The camera couldn't see them either.

His phone rang, startling him and cutting through the silence in his studio. It was Lucky Star. They were probably wondering where the hell he was. He declined to answer; he couldn't go back out with everything that had just been revealed. He should have just ordered out in the first place. If he had just gone with the fucking pizza, he could have completely avoided the whole mess. Instead, he was treated to an awful sinking feeling inside like his heart was in quicksand.

Maybe he was overthinking everything, he just needed to lay low for a few more days and this whole episode would just blow over. If he stopped thinking about it, he would stop giving it power. Pizza and video games sounded really good to him right now.

He placed the order online at the only spot to order a pie from in his opinion, Lord's Pizza. They had the best crust and always delivered quickly. He settled on two large meat lovers and a matching pair of bubbly two-liter cokes.

If this was to be his last meal, he wanted to do it right. He wanted his favorite. The thought of their tangy tomato sauce smothered in a heap of melting cheese with more dead animals entrenched in it than he could count just felt so right.

He fired up the flat screen and then picked up his controller. He decided to shift his schedule slightly, playing video games could wait until he ate. He didn't want to stop his play midway; he preferred to wait for his food first and then start. He was a man that would avoid greasy joysticks. Instead, he switched the input and allowed the TV to help him separate from the issues at hand.

He drifted off in his mind, closing his eyes, blocking out the abundance of negative shit the news-casters continued to cram down the throats of their audience. He was bordering on a meditative state, keeping his canvas as blank as possible. Only seeing a blank canvas, leaving no room for anything else.

He'd done this many times before to clear his head. Then, slowly, he would add different things to the portrait of a positive nature. The first thing he chose to add was some of the elusive steaming, fresh beef fried rice from Lucky Star. Next, the rice was joined with the most golden, crisp-looking chicken fingers he could imagine.

This stuff looked amazing but that was just the warm-up. A 20-inch Lord's meat lovers hovered down beside the Lucky Star, spinning mesmerizingly like some sort of delicious UFO. Closing his eyes to imagine food made him feel kind of like a fat ass but it was better than the other, more pressing alternatives. His daze was cut short by a gentle knock at the door, the pizza dude was finally there.

He ran to the closet and snatched his wallet out of his inside pocket. The guiltiest of pleasure had made its way to him. Soon, the madness encountered today would make little difference. Soon, he would have a warm pie steaming below his jaw as it rattled with excitement. He made his way over to the door, enthusiastically popping the deadbolt and removing the sliding chain.

As he listened to the old hinge draw open, his face held the kind of delight you might see upon a child at the local Chuck E. Cheese's. It shifted rapidly as what was revealed next was something he'd failed to consider altogether. Something that the fat kid in him overlooked due to a hunger for the reassuring garbage we all crave for comfort.

Instead of eating the repulsive cream of mushroom soup he had in his cupboard for unknown reasons, he was now confronted with the impossible frozen at his doorstep. He was face to face with the Vortex Man, who was now oddly dressed in the angelic Lord's Pizza uniform that he'd come to find great relief in seeing. The uniform that always received a good tip and provided him with evenings of bliss had now taken a completely different form from the stoners that normally rocked it.

Now it was modeled by the spiky-haired 20-something-year-old that couldn't be staring at him because his eyes were glued shut. That they were, but somehow Martin still sensed that the man was acutely aware. Just like the photo he'd downloaded, his nose appeared fluid, this sort of constant running river that trickled down to a honeydew melon-sized vortex hovering inside his chin and throat.

The wormhole was a deep purple on the edges, turning into a midnight black toward the center that seemed to stretch forward for eternity like a hallway in a funhouse mirror would. There was an electric humming sound, in addition to a kind of static that might be produced from an old tube television.

The Vortex Man looked to be cannibalizing himself in a strange, digital way. His literal running nose spiraled as it descended back into him. Twisting into the obscure before being consumed into the vortex altogether. He had done all he could to escape it but somehow his worst fear had found him.

Martin was unable to move. Not because of his own fear or anything that was within his control to break free of, but because of something else entirely. A force so powerful it was beyond his comprehension. He tried with everything to move his legs and step away but they simply wouldn't work.

Seconds later, even having the thought of moving was no longer possible. His mind blanked out, wiped clean of any inkling or any of its most rudimentary past abilities. His eyes now fixated on the pulsating darkness as it circled before him, but only for another instant. His vision was the next thing that was taken. It turned off swiftly like someone had put a black garbage bag over his head in the middle of the night.

The last thing Martin felt was an incredible, violent suction that drew his flesh and bones forward. A heavy crushing pain resonated throughout what was left of him, even his already swallowed areas. He would have killed to scream, to have a way to express the dread that he could no longer think about but still somehow felt. Unfortunately, at this point, screaming and crying were faculties that he'd been stripped of. He was now at the mercy of the Vortex.

Doreen entered the La Grange Cafe, which was known for providing a quiet and comforting setting in Paris's normally hectic Latin District. She ordered a coffee, not in the irritating overly specific way that most people around there did. Providing about a paragraph worth of instruction had somehow become commonplace. She grabbed the steaming beverage once it was finished and found a cozy seat with a nice buffer zone away from others in the corner.

She popped open her laptop and unlocked it while taking a sip of her coffee. Her desktop was a spliced together version of various Warcraft and Diablo characters. She grazed over their faces with her mouse before opening her email. She noticed the most recent notification was from a close friend and selected it first, curious about the contents. It read:

"Doreen, you must look at this site, when I initially saw it, I knew you would find hours of amusement on it. The website is: www.thispersondoesnotexist.com

Tell me if you think this is real or what you make of it. Each time you refresh the site, it updates with a different person. I still haven't figured out if they really exist or not yet but one thing is for certain, they look incredibly real. Have fun, Bridgette."

Doreen paused only a fraction of a moment after reading the note. Bridgette was right, the title alone was irresistible to her. She quickly clicked the link and waited with anticipation for her browser to load. The only thing that came up was a single picture of what looked like a deformed man.

His curly black hair seemed like the kind that was just impossible to style or make look decent. His facial hair was inconsistent patches of beard growing in different places as if the individual had not quite hit puberty yet.

His face looked like that of a depressed man in his 30s. The most disturbing part was the creepy purple and black blob around his chin and throat area, she couldn't seem to stop staring at it. She got the chills but couldn't help but be completely transfixed by the creepy image. Something about it was calling to her for reasons beyond her understanding.

She decided she would need to share this with Bridgette before she refreshed to see the next one. She began to wonder if Bridgette might have seen any of these black hole glitches in the people that she generated on the site. She smiled, feeling at ease, knowing she'd found something unique to entertain her on her day off. Doreen cheerfully right-clicked on Martin's image and downloaded it.

CLUB HELL

Ah, the early 20s, there is no other period quite like it. For the vast majority, it's unforgettable, usually an era in which people's lives are infested with the fragmented recollections of the "good times" that required a lot of glue (or a sober witness) to assemble.

Well, at least most of the memories started out good, but more often than not, ended at the house of some creepy stranger or cleaning vomit off the floor of the car the following morning. You might have cleaned it, but you still couldn't escape the smell for a few days. That was the smell of youth… and maybe a little bile and whiskey too.

Near-death experiences, high-risk situations, and horrible, sometimes trajectory shifting decisions were what people in that era were often faced with. The morning after being the ultimate of uncertain stretches one would be challenged with.

When given the license to drink and surrounded by friends with drugs, every night is a party. It was all about finding a way to beat the last high, cutting it just a little bit closer and gradually becoming more reckless with each approaching weekend. What the hell, right? You're only 21 for a year.

That was Celeste's exact sentiment. She'd grown tired of playing the good girl. She was the type that obtained straight As with regularity and always played it safe. Her parents were strict on her in a most overbearing style. They saw to it that she kept it conservative and respectful.

Their intention was honest enough, they'd do anything to avoid seeing her bungle a promising future. Ironically, in the end, their plan would boomerang. The stringency of the restrictive lifestyle they'd fostered caused Celeste to rebel, in turn, triggering her to piss away the educational opportunities that she'd worked incredibly hard to earn.

She was presented a plethora of valuable scholarships but decided that, instead of pursuing further education, she'd already had her fill of it. She threw up two slender middle fingers the way of her folks and the preordained path they'd constructed for her. She'd be making her own path now.

They were stunned when she literally told them to "Fuck off" on her eighteenth birthday, before moving out shortly thereafter. Horrified by this personality shift, they scolded her to no avail. She was done fearing them. Afterward, she drew up a formal letter to each school on expensive, high-quality paper. Each had a finely arranged header and provided a two-word response to the college offers. The same final two words she'd sought fit for her parents.

She'd decided instead that she was long overdue for some real-life experiences outside of the soft safe-space bubble of the educational system and surely outside of her control-freak parents' house.

Throwing her whole future away felt great, mainly because it's something she was doing. For the first time in her life, she was calling the shots. She would continue the job she'd been working since high school as a barista at the Bean Connection, a large coffee shop downtown. But to stay afloat and pay the bills, she'd be upgraded to a full-time first shift position.

Her manager, Ben, was flabbergasted by her bid, but at the same time, thrilled. If he could have hired five more of her, he would have. She was the best worker in the building. Getting her full-time only made his life easier.

Her coworker, Adriana, would be her first roommate. She'd been in talks about taking the spare room in her apartment. This would be a logical change for many reasons, the primary being that Adriana was continuously just scraping by. With Celeste moving in, she would not only have her girl around to chill with all the time but it would free up some cash for her so they could do some real partying.

Inadvertently, it was Adriana who'd inspired Celeste to modify her future. Listening to her countless stories of late-night insanity had left her with a harsh case of the millennial disease, FOMO (fear of missing out).

College would always be there, but acting retarded for a few years of her youth wouldn't. She needed to have these experiences, she needed to make mistakes to find out what the hell actually mattered to her in life. At the moment, all she had was someone else's version of what her life should be, but the brainwashing was about to end.

Adriana was a spicy Colombian girl that Celeste considered to be her best friend. She had a sexy, curvy but not overweight body and lovely, typically wet, curly blonde hair that blended intentionally with her dark attractive roots.

She administered her make-up with perfect strategy, never over-applying it. She perfected her craft to the point where she could make herself and Celeste both look like models when they went out (granted, she always did Celeste's make-up just a little bit shittier than her own).

Although Adriana probably wouldn't admit it to their larger circle, she viewed Celeste as her BFF too. She thought Celeste was a cool girl that didn't really conflict with her philosophies, more importantly, she was less hot so she didn't feel threatened.

It was always a foregone conclusion that if the pair was out, Adriana was always getting matched up with the hotter guy. Sure, Adriana was a bitch but only when the stars didn't align. Thankfully, the basic rules of attraction and Celeste's easygoing nature made their relationship work effortlessly.

They had been two peas in a pod for a few years and their carousel binge felt never-ending, more like they'd been doing it for ten years rather than three. However, there was a method to their madness, they were on the verge of a very important milestone. One which would always be the pinnacle of their raging youth. It was everything they'd been talking about for so long now, the event that was legendary and once in a lifetime. Turning 21.

Up until that point, all of the carousing they'd been doing had been strictly confined to house parties. They had not been able to pierce into the wild club scene that downtown constantly dangled before them. The endless tease of stories they'd heard, the euphoria they'd been drooling over for years, was nearly upon them.

Others downplayed the events they'd been a part of as amateur, even boring, compared to what these immoral, degenerate establishments offered. Adriana was turning 21 that Friday and they both knew it was finally time to either confirm or dismiss the hype. To be reborn and burst into the most wicked of scenes.

Celeste had already turned 21 a few months ago but made a pact with Adriana that she would wait for her to pop their cherries together. An undeniable excitement was in the air at the coffee shop that day.

Ben could see something was up with the girls. They were far chattier and less focused on the customers than usual and staring at the clock neurotically, or "wall watching" as he called it. He wasn't privy to their priorities but couldn't help but wonder what had the girls so riled up.

"So, what is it? You guys just going to buzz around for the last half an hour and not tell me?" Ben cracked.

Celeste finished wiping up the counter, the place was pretty much dead at that hour. "Should we tell him?" she asked, looking to Adriana.

"It's my birthday, didn't you know?" she replied.

"Of course, I know, who do you think bought your cake? You two almost seem a little nervous, I'm sure that has nothing to do with your birthday," he said, prying a bit further.

"We're going out tonight, we're going to the club for the first time!" she screeched, wrapping her arm around Celeste giddily.

"Oh, God, are you guys kidding me, the club? You realize those places are just filled with creeps, right? Creeps that'll all be vying for the privilege to roofie your drink the first time you blink."

"I know, we're gonna get so much attention!" Adriana said, delighted, not fully understanding the idea Ben was putting on the table.

"We'll watch our drinks, we're big girls, Ben, it's not like we haven't been to a party before," Celeste assured him.

"Yeah, but the breed of slime ball in these places, you have no idea. Where are you going?"

"Downtown. We were thinking Therapy maybe?" Celeste replied.

"That's probably what you'll need after a night in there," he quipped.

"That place sucks, you don't wanna go there." Another female voice said from behind them.

The conversation turned to Zoey; she'd clearly overheard them en route back from cleaning the tables. The girls weren't particularly fond of Zoey but didn't completely despise her either.

She was a couple of years their senior and had a more depressing, gothic aura about her. It was as if her additional life experiences had weighed her down a bit. Her partially dreadlocked hair was usually arranged a little different each day and was smattered with a hint of blue dye. The array of steel ball and bar piercings was a perfect complement to her pale body that was tattooed to excess.

The inked art was repulsive and offensive, about what you'd expect from a girl who only watched splatter movies and pulled up to the premises blasting Cannibal Corpse. She was a bit of an acquired taste but certainly interesting if nothing else.

"You two have been talking about this for months, so do you wanna go to a real club tonight or what?"

Adriana didn't like to feel like anyone knew something she didn't, but at the same time, she was more than intrigued, so she let Celeste field the inquiry.

"Like where?" Celeste asked.

"I can get us into Hell," Zoey replied.

"What's that?" she prodded.

"Zoey! Don't take them to Club Hell, it's their first time," Ben cautioned.

"Ben, you may be the boss of our bean bar here, but outside, in the real world, they get to decide for themselves," Zoey explained, pulling him back down to earth.

Ben's disapproval really made going to Hell seem much more appealing for them. They had no idea what Club Hell was but it was almost as if they didn't care. The name was salacious enough. Adriana stepped forward a bit, straightening up as if she was making an epic decision.

"We're in."

"That place is nothing more than a depraved fetish bar, it's a cesspool full of freaks and addicts," Ben remarked, trying to sway them.

"Don't try and spoil it for others just cuz you can't get in, Ben. The jealousy comes off as pathetic. It's a venomous thing, like an infection, it'll spread through you quickly."

"I can get into Hell, who are you kidding?" he defended.

"That's true, Ben. But not until you're dead. Girls, meet me out front after we close, we're gonna tear shit up tonight, I promise you that."

The girls had picked up a handle of vodka on the way home. They could drink as much as they pleased with minimal calories. They had a few hours before they were meeting Zoey downtown. The clubs didn't really get going until ten or eleven, so they had plenty of time to perfect their outfits, make-up, and pregame.

Zoey had told them to dress like sluts if they wanted to get in and as they modeled their potential outfits, they both edged each other to a trashier, darker place. They continued to throw back shots throughout this process, neglecting to pace themselves. The abundance of booze paired with the mega doses of Adderall they'd swallowed had them looking more like they were wearing Halloween costumes as opposed to dressing up. Either way their outfits worked.

By the time they were supposed to head out, they were in full asylum mode, bouncing off the walls and speaking with a Bone Thugs-n-Harmony swiftness. Adriana ended up in a nylon shirt, with only pasties covering her see-through top. Her shredded jean shorts left the curves of her ass exposed and made her bronzed legs seem to stretch on forever.

Attempting to balance herself in the tall spiked heels that registered at a breakneck height was difficult now, so in a few hours, it would be damn near impossible she imagined. That challenge failed to push her to switch her selection. She was too focused on applying the finest cosmetic layers that Celeste had ever seen, although she'd gone a more sinister route this time, laying on the eye shadow in abundance.

Celeste's outfit looked closer to a dominatrix. In

fact, she was wearing an old latex onesie that she'd bought at the request of her ex. The shine glistened fiercely, her cleavage busting out of the outfit, it was fitting a bit tighter than before. Her frayed pantyhose was a nice complement to her steampunk-esque calf climbing black boots that were each littered with unnecessary buckles.

Her black gloves reached up to the elbow and she clenched a prairie horse leather flogger in her left hand. The collective garments presented her like some kind of Betty Page throwback with an extra touch of skank. They were both certain the freakshow they'd be at the center of tonight would be ready to eat them up. The fact that they had no idea what to expect excited them the most.

When they arrived downtown, Zoey was already outside smoking a cigarette, seemingly on a heavy dose of something far harder than what they'd consumed. Her head was swaying back and forth, while she stood alone but only a few feet away from a larger group.

A cluster of wiggers had found a pair of "ladies" that seemed to be interested in them. So much so that they were peeling up their tight skirts and fingering them vigorously. The problem seemed to arise when they began to notice some of their more masculine qualities.

"You ain't no fuckin bitch!" the South Pole clad white boy screamed.

The fist-fight stirred up quickly with one of the trannies punching the loud mouth in the face, bloodying him. But the pack of wiggers descended on them like wolves, savagely beating them to the pavement, whereupon they began stomping their heads into the concrete.

It was clear that it was going to be a long night. The girls grabbed Zoey by the arm and dragged her toward the back of the line and away from the melee. It took them a few cracks to garner a response from her but, eventually, it came.

"Listen to me, you both shut the fuck up and let me do the talking," she commanded, slurring her speech.

They concurred non-verbally as the line of undesirables dwindled, pulling them closer and closer toward the entrance. A short time later, they were in front of a very terrifying, very bald, very pierced bouncer. He stared a hole through them, speechless, the element that they appeared to be ladies meant nothing to him. His courtesies had died long ago.

"Let us in," Zoey demanded in a cold manner.

"Why should I let a fucking laced cunt like you in?" he asked, patience already clearly tested.

"Because if you don't, I'll tell Psycho. You know if he doesn't get what he wants, he's not going to be very happy with you."

"And what does he want?" he asked, lending a bit of credence to her statements.

"Me."

He considered it for a moment before opening the curtain for them. The three girls marched forward, thirsty for a strong drink. The bouncer extended his arm in front of Celeste and Adriana, blatantly rubbing against their tits and pulling them back toward him.

"The pigs stay!" he barked.

"He wants the pigs too, retard!" she screamed, her earsplitting pitch causing him to bounce back.

"Let's go!" Zoey yelled, throwing her arms up victoriously, directing the girls to trail behind her.

They forced their way into the dreary hall, faces

mashed with the scent of stuffy, stagnant air that stunk of smoke, vomit, and potent body odor. The music was rumbling the foundation and the volume turned up to Spinal Tap standards. Moving forward, they'd have to scream to communicate with each other, which made for almost no change to Zoey's standard tone.

The red and black lights attached to the stage were pulsating and flailing about in a trippy way. Illuminating the band and projecting their shadows across a blood-stained backdrop. Their spiked instruments produced a demonic-sounding metal that cut into the soul.

They thrashed their heads repeatedly as if possessed, while sweat flung off their drenched long hair into the group of listeners assaulting each other below them. A body lay on the floor leaking profusely and motionless.

It was hard to tell if it was a boy or a girl that had been clobbered, their gothic attire created more mystery than explanation. It was also hard to tell if they were dead or alive. The evil crowd was energized and unremorseful for the scene displayed. Celeste and Adriana watched the creeps continue their vehemence, psychotically stomping their combat boots before a member of the flock unzipped his jeans and pissed on the lifeless body.

"These people are fuckin' crazy!" Celeste said, cupping her hand around Adriana's ear.

"We got ourselves into something tonight!" she responded, clearly more excited by the danger than her counterpart.

The music was laced with dark electronic synths, in addition to the gain cranked, speedy power-chords. The singer's words were indecipherable but the throat-ripping screams he bellowed out helped the listener understand this tune wasn't aimed to please.

The girls nudged up against the bar in the only area that was available. The vacancy on the aged wooden slab they could probably thank the last patron for, whoever had graced the area blew chunks and nastiness all over it. What an appropriate place to order their first drink.

"What do you want?" Zoey asked in her usual annoyed for unknown reasons tone.

The two girls looked at each other for a minute, almost shrugging before turning back to her.

"Ketel?" they said in chorus.

"People don't drink fucking Ketel here. You're in Hell, remember? I'm going to order us a real drink, the house special, it'll knock your socks off, I promise. And since I got you two bitches in, I'd imagine you'd express your gratitude by buying me at least one drink," Zoey snarked.

"Fine, whatever," Celeste replied, growing more tired of her "only I know the cool things" attitude.

Zoey observed the pasty-faced bartender whose dead eyes did not really look at her, more through her.

"Three Devil's Blood," she said, symbolizing the number with her fingers, while the bartender left without responding.

"Devil's Blood, what exactly is Devil's Blood?" Adriana asked.

"Honey, relax. Okay? Nothing that you haven't come across during your little trips back to your homeland."

The bartender returned with three glasses that sat in the palm of a demon claw that was the shade of gargoyle. A blackish, red fluid sat inside unwavering.

"One-eighty," the bartender yelled out, void of emotion.

"One-eighty, that can't be right. We only ordered three drinks," Celeste squawked.

"One-eighty!" the bartender screamed back, slamming her fist down, causing the glasses on the bar to jump slightly.

"Oh, girls, you don't wanna know what happens if you don't pay. Trust me, this is not the kind of place to toy around in," Zoey said in her best shit-stirring voice.

Adriana looked dumbfounded while she watched Celeste pull out the cash to cover the exorbitant tab. The normally outspoken bad-ass of their tandem seemed like she was in over her head. They both were.

She pulled out the other half of the cash and slammed it down beside Celeste's. She was finally getting her nerve up, her blood boiling with her eyes now locked on Zoey.

"This is ridiculous, we said we'd buy you a drink not the whole fuckin' bar, bitch. What's your problem anyway? You realize that's pretty much all the money we brought, right!? And we only have one drink!" she screamed, her spit splashing on Zoey's cheeks.

"You only need one of these," she answered with an annoying giggle.

"Let's take a lap," she said, picking up her drink and moving away from the bar.

The girls did the only thing they could at that point—grabbed their drinks and followed. They entangled themselves with the army of grinding bodies on the gloomy dance floor.

It felt like a swamp except filled with flesh that was pulling you down like a thick marshland. They pushed their way through, trying not to spill their drinks, fending off people's (men, women, and only God knows what) hands from the constant groping of their more intimate parts.

The group all seemed to be salivating with carnal modus, a dark animalistic aggressiveness unified them. Others danced mindlessly; the agony settled upon their faces so convincingly but it had to be a bluff. They were dancing, no one is sad when they dance, are they?

"Why are these goth kids all so damn miserable? Who dances with a face like that?!" Adriana yelled at Celeste while they twisted through the crowd.

"This place is weird, where are we going?!" Celeste shouted back.

"Zoey's gotta take a dump!"

When they arrived at the ladies' room, they were greeted by a strictly homosexual version of the human centipede that was partially blocking the entrance. Three boys that couldn't be a day over 18 all connected together by only cock and asshole.

They were all stripped down save for the boy in the front who was bent over a metal railing wearing a Bright Eyes t-shirt. It was hard to tell if he was enjoying it, as he was completely passed out, crimson running down the legs of his suitor.

"Can't you faggots read? This is the ladies' room! Find somewhere else to give each other AIDS!" she said, tossing the malnourished boy aside.

They filed into the restroom which was a whole different landmark of disturbed. Every fluid or filth imaginable had overrun the entire room, layer upon layer of the sickest shit the human body could expel.

Two of the seven stalls had been ripped down. The first exposed toilet was filled with a deep red fluid and dripping wet. The second one had the seat torn off and its porcelain lip had an enormous portion that had been smashed away.

Feces smeared around the rear and also filled the bowl as if it had gone a month without someone tugging the handle. The place was throwing an aroma that had Adriana gagging, trying desperately to keep her lunch down. The smell was nasty but what was more mortifying were the visuals.

A punk girl with a blue mullet and shredded jean jacket was passed out on her knees with the tip of her skull dipped inside the mess.

"Is she... is she dead?" Celeste asked nervously.

"Who gives a fuck? I gotta take a shit," Zoey said, pulling her limp body out of the bowl.

The girl toppled over beside the john and her skull cracked loudly, splashing in a puddle of urine on the checkered floor. Zoey picked the wet, broken toilet seat up from the side of the bowl and set it where it would normally rest. She didn't bother to wipe it off before sitting on it, or take her panties off, mainly because she wasn't wearing any.

The girls were repulsed with each growing minute they spent with Zoey, but what could they do? She was their lifeline tonight. Zoey elevated her glass toward them in an effort to celebrate, they hesitated slightly before accepting her offer.

"Alright, girls, it's time to put these away and cheers to a couple of young, dumb but sexy skanks like yourselves, going to Hell, finding out what the fuck life is really about!"

They banged glasses before downing them completely, despite Zoey's moronic and disrespectful toast. The girls both shuddered as the warm, thick liquid crawled its way down their esophagi.

The taste of aged black licorice and rot intertwining upon their pallets was overpowering when paired with the increasingly more atrocious illustrations around them, it's a wonder they were able to put it away. Zoey seemed fine, like she'd enjoyed the putrid flavor. A long smile sliced its way across her face and she started to shit her brains out.

"Ugggghhhh! What the fuck was that!?" Adriana blurted out, rinsing out her glass in the sink and trying to refill it with water.

"What kind of mixed drink is warm and thick? It tastes like the shitty candy my grandmother gives out," Celeste chimed in, a little more reserved.

You could still hear the disgusting sound effects of the moist log exiting Zoey's canal when she answered them.

"You know why I like absinthe? It's because it has a little sin in the middle, just like me. Probably shouldn't drink while I'm pregnant, but fuck it, if it's meant to be, I'm sure it'll survive," Zoey said, rubbing her stomach.

Suddenly, everything slowed down for them, the visuals began to bend, the walls now seemed alive like they were the meat covering a giant pair of lungs pushing their surroundings to a rhythmic pulsation. A terrifying idea in a structure that oozed an undeniably diabolical aura.

"What did we just take? Oh shit... Adriana, I'm fucked," Celeste admitted, listening to her own words echo somehow.

"Guess you never had wormwood before. You know, it really can't make you hallucinate at all, but whatever else they mix with it sure as shit can," she said, ending with a cackle that repeated with slight delay throughout their eardrums.

The girls were too wasted to comprehend the things that Zoey found so hysterical to divulge to them. Adriana was busy staring at herself in the mirror, her beautiful make-up seemed to be running off her face now. Like a river of caramel cosmetics dripping into the grimy sink beneath her.

She grabbed a few paper towels from the mangled dispenser beside her and began to wipe her cheeks off aggressively, as if this would somehow help the issue. With each wipe, she turned a little redder but she ignored it, only paying attention to the urge… and the urge was to keep wiping.

Celeste was now also deeply concerned with the red toilet. The bowl of blood seemed to bubble before her, massaging the assortment of used tampons from every bleeding club rat in the state. *Why the fuck is it moving like that? It can't just move on its own, it's not alive, right?* She wondered.

Her questions would have to wait, her attention turned to her screaming friend. Adriana's cheeks were now raw and gory from the ferocious rubbing, she was seeing maggots peeking in and out of the aggravated skin. Her attempts had moved from wiping off beauty aids to removing slimy larva from her jawline in a matter of moments.

"What's wrong!?" Celeste shrieked, trying to understand her while Zoey snickered behind them.

The group's attention would soon be drawn from all of their internal mental horrors to an amplified real-life version. The stall door beside them burst open, flying clean off the hinges. A man, they could only assume, stepped out.

His whole frame was nude but concealed by the

litter of straight, grungy hair that coated every inch of his body. He looked more like a gorilla than a human, his jaw unhinged and frothing rabidly as his fangs protruded through the foamy drool. The girls were frozen in disbelief and dread, battling for dominance in their brains. A calm seemed to come over the ape man as he closed his jaws and took a step closer.

"You know, it's really hard to go in there with you guys screaming like that," he surprised them with a gentlemanly posture as he pointed toward the stall he'd just burst out of.

The girls looked at each other wide-eyed while Zoey seemed as if she wasn't paying attention.

"And what's wrong with her?" he asked, gesturing toward the unconscious girl laying in the giant puddle of piss.

Celeste and Adriana's screeches blared out and were about as shrill as you might expect. Pupils still locked, Celeste then grabbed her by the wrist and ran, leading them out of the wacky and nightmarish room.

They expected at least an instant of remission from the mind-bending roller-coaster they'd hopped on, but it wasn't in the cards. It became apparent that when the Devil's Blood was in you, there were no breaks or escape. They watched everything they knew become a question mark. Their sanity and composure shattering before them into more pieces than you could count and the seven years of bad luck had already kicked off free of charge.

The light display was both petrifying and mesmerizing, like an inescapable fire of colors had engulfed the room. It meshed and danced in and out of the hot ocean of perversion that licked them and latched on as they became one with the mauling hands again. It was mostly just bloodshot eyes and distorted fingers that jumped out as they continued onward. A dark haze curtained the dance floor around them, they began to lose control.

Entrenched in the sea of humanity, the eyes seemed to be angrier now. A brighter white light illuminated more than just the gateways to the souls of the deranged dancers. The girls were now seeing what they really were, and their gateways had disintegrated long ago. Their prior mirage had lifted, unveiling them as the soulless subspecies that they were while casting their countless hostile stares upon Celeste and Adriana.

The dancers were chiseled into what felt like impossible dimensions for a mortal canvas to be tasked with displaying. Stretched facial skin hung out, sometimes the length of a ruler, defying gravity as there couldn't be any bone inside to help keep it splinted.

The monstrous clay-like abominations sat skin bubbling on the surface, not fit for those of sound mind to view. Their features molded to a permanent look of disdain, as if the frenzied appearance they bore was never-ending. Mother had told them that if they kept making that face, it would stick that way.

They were showing them the teeth now, sharp and yellow, inflamed meat impaled and stuck between some of them. They seemed like they were just growing in immensity, either that or getting closer. They wondered if their own meat might end up destined for a toothpick. The thoughts were interrupted when the girls each felt a hand on their backs, pushing them forward through the demons with a strength that seemed more refined than Zoey's.

A short time later, they were detached from the demonic mosh-pit of famished freaks and passed the bar into a small office. The iron numbers "666" sat over the cardinal-colored, half-cracked door. The hands guided them to a seat, a long leather therapist sofa is where they stopped to rest. The lighting in the room felt out of a pulp detective novel as they both laid back, still trying to move past the prior angst stirring inside them.

As they lifted their heavy heads up to find their savior, they noticed a bright light emanating from behind the figure, the kind you might see noticeably outlined around a saint in a Catholic oil painting. The shape took another stride forward under the focused ceiling light, its attributes now perceivable to them.

He was a beautiful but rough-looking man. His fearless, sharpened looks were complemented by his manly gristle, just the kind of person to protect them from the torment outside the walls of the calm office. His black jeans and tank top were covered by his sangria-toned leather jacket.

The tattoos that leaked out of the areas where his skin was visible seemed to be crawling at the pace of a tortoise, but not in a manner that disturbed the girls. This man did not have to smile to project his good spirits, they could physically feel it.

"I'm Psycho," he said, laying out the introduction in a voice meant for radio.

The girls continued to sit motionless, unsure of how to convey what they felt, what had happened before and, more importantly, what they wanted to happen next. After a few more ticks, it clicked that this was the guy Zoey used as her clout to gain them entry. How many guys could be named Psycho? Maybe more than they initially thought in a place like this.

"I'm guessing you tried the Devil's Blood?" he said with a laugh.

Celeste mustered up the composure to nod her head a few times, although she still looked like she wasn't necessarily responding to him.

"Well, I own this place," he said, craning a drink up from his desk and taking a sip. "I haven't seen you here before and I've got a pretty keen eye, so this must be your first time. I know this place can be... well, over the years, it's evolved into something a bit chaotic. The clientele has just really stretched the limits of acceptability. But at the same time, here we really like to feed off our freedoms, to do essentially whatever it is we please. I saw the two of you seemed a bit buried out there. I wanted to offer you entry into a different area of the club. Somewhere not so muddled, somewhere that the chaos is a little more... focused, shall we say."

His smile was marvelous. They'd been lost inside it since he began. The words he chose seemed sweet and thoughtful, although they couldn't comprehend them. The conversation was cut short by a pounding on the door so rugged that the artwork on the walls jumped.

Psycho excused himself to answer the door. As he opened it a quarter of the way, Zoey wormed herself inside prior to any question or communication.

She didn't notice the girls sitting on the couch and got down on her knees. She had a piece of toilet tissue hanging from inside her skirt with (presumably her) shit caked on it, as she started to unzip his jeans.

"Well, don't you want to say hi to your friends first, darling?" Psycho asked her.

Zoey gazed over, pausing her promiscuity, a bit excited.

"There you are! I was looking everywhere for you two," she cried, seeming to emit a kind of compassion that would have been more likely to come from Hitler before her.

"Yes, in fact, I was just explaining to them about the VIP parties that we hold downstairs. So much better than all the madness you've been bombarded with thus far, wouldn't you say?" Psycho rehashed.

"My ladies are coming. This is their first night not just at a club, but THE club. I wouldn't be a very good friend if I let them miss it, would I?"

The elevator ride was silent and nauseating. They were still so fucked up, it was hard to tell if they were going up or down. It should have been a short trip considering the entry point of the club was street level, but that wasn't the case. There was no digital readout in the elevator. The edges were surrounded by a fencing that you could see through, more akin to a freight elevator than a traditional one. An orange glow reached up from below, laying over the old hand that pointed from left to right at the variety of floors.

"How many floors are in this fucking place?" Celeste pondered, still staggered by the drugs. It became clearer that they were descending as the hand dipped deeper to the left. A defective sounding ding rang out about every twenty seconds or so.

Zoey kissed Psycho and grabbed his cock firmly with her pale fingers, jerking it slightly. It may have been in part that they were influenced by whatever was in the drink but it felt like an hour had passed when the metal platform screeched to a halt.

The door opened to a wall of curtain the shade of eggplant. They penetrated the fabric, feeling the warm amber glow begin to peek out. They were blinded as they stepped through, they could see what looked like a few hundred stone steps with the light perched atop.

The edges of the steps were plagued with an innumerable amount of bones and skulls, many were impaled with large knives driven through them.

Beyond those was a steep fall into more of the tangerine nothingness, anguish-riddled groans lingered up from the depths.

The girls had no explanation for what they were witnessing, the inconceivable barefaced before them, their lives forever changed. At the edges of the curtains were a myriad of multi-jointed hands protruding from the jagged stone walls behind them.

Two of them accordioned their way to the girls from the back and quickly administered a crushing grip that ejected their oxygen like one would sitting on a whoopee cushion. As the grip tightened, Zoey laughed beside Psycho who maintained his composure.

The girls began to sob and cry, unknowing of the events that would soon transpire; however, they were more than certain they would be unpleasant. Their cries continued to become louder and louder, and for the first time, Psycho appeared a little annoyed.

"Well, we've got a solution for this, don't we now," he said, placing his hand over Zoey's stomach.

Immediately, she began trembling and convulsing, she fell to the ground shaking violently and holding her gut. The blood shot out of her like puss would from a zit, painting the floor below her.

What came out with the mess was difficult to describe. It looked repulsive like a slimy, steaming sand-worm covered in fluid. It was long enough to stretch out about eight feet as each end of it slithered its way up the girls' slutty outfits.

Eventually, it inserted the many chattering mouths housed on each end of itself halfway down their throats, causing their necks to bulge and throb like some kind of absurd porn gif.

"Ah, quiet at last. Thank God," Psycho said, quite

relieved by the notion.

An ominous roar shook their foundation with a force that almost caused him to topple over the edge and into the nothingness.

"Right, not a fan. You know what I meant," Psycho said, looking up the cracked staircase.

"Let that be a lesson, ladies. Watch what you say around here," he joked.

Psycho walked up a couple of the stairs, kicking some of the old bones off the fringe and watching them fall down the nearby pit. He then removed one of the long blades that were lodged into a corpse and the stone beneath it, and crept back toward them.

He looked down at Zoey. She remained out cold, still idle save for the abnormally thick river of carnage creeping slowly forward from between her legs.

"Now, I suppose I have to ask. Who wants to see Botis first?" he inquired. The girls could only gag on their worm, a response was hardly possible. "Forgive me. You're still a bit tongue-tied, aren't you now? Blink twice to volunteer please," he stared at them patiently, awaiting the response as both girls strained to keep their eyes open.

"Okay, I guess we want to be difficult. Let me demonstrate what's going to happen to you if we don't get a volunteer shortly." He bent over slightly, grabbing a clump of Zoey's dreads to elevate her up. She remained slumped over, her seepage still spilling out methodically as he raised the blade.

"See, right here, we have just another stupid bitch. A real cunt that brainwashed herself to believe she was an integral part of this sinister domain we run. In reality though, she's really more disposable than the cloth she inserts into herself at the end of the month," he explained.

Still, neither girl blinked as he drove the blade into her neck, effortlessly slicing through the spine and tissue in one swift motion. The skin casing ripped as her body crumpled back to the floor, she was now leaking from both ends. Psycho tossed the skull over his head, spilling a blood trail over his once pristine jacket.

"You made me get my hands dirty now. It's okay, I don't mind doing the wet work, how do you think I got this gig?"

As he finished the question, he drove the blade into Zoey's asshole, pushing deeper and deeper down the center, pulling upward until her nether region had been partially filleted. He then moved onto dismembering her, cutting each limb off and tossing it into the depths.

Eventually, all that was left was a puddle of nastiness and a few sections of torso. The tears had been draining from the girls with a frequency that left depression trails of mascara rampaging over their cheeks. Still, neither of them had closed their eyelids.

"Oh no, here come the water works. Listen, I'm gonna give you two one more chance on the blink thing. Let's see someone step up and be a big girl for me," he offered again, this time swinging the drenched sword like he was imitating a samurai.

Adriana finally gave way, not just the accidental, biology breakdown blink like she'd lost a staring contest. She'd done so with intent, ready to take one for the team. She blinked a second time.

Immediately, Psycho sliced the area of the worm closest to her mouth. An orangey solution rained out as the piece that was already inside her throat disappeared down into her stomach. She hurled a few times but that fucker wasn't leaving. She could feel its teeth clamped down and piercing into her innards.

"What the fuck are you doing?!" she screamed hysterically.

"Now, calm down a minute—"

"W—What is this place?" she asked sobbing.

"Oh, there are SO many names, and if I'm being truthful, you're in no position to be demanding answers, miss. But let me humor you a little. You ate the worm. I suppose it's the least I can do. What if I told you that after a lifetime of eating fried foods or shooting dope, or just plain old boring existence, whenever your little heart decides to pack it in, that hell isn't somewhere you just POOF magically appear at? That it's not just for pedophiles or the sick fucks and murderers? What if I told you that we already live in hell, it just depends on how far you're willing to go to find it. See, it's just like any other place, there're a few ways in, they're just concealed really well, kind of like the repulsive divots in your fucking face that you've so carefully disguised. It doesn't change the fact that they're there though and any morning you could wake up and see them. Today, you just happened to be superbly unfortunate."

"Please, please let me go, I just wanna go back, please," Adriana begged and pleaded.

"I wish I could do something to help you. Really, my heart aches for you. Sadly though, I'm not the head honcho here. Well, ascetically maybe I am. I pay the bills, take the complaints and whatnot, but that doesn't mean shit. Botis up there, he's the one that can do it all. He can make your nightmares a reality," he said, aiming the sword up the stairwell toward the light.

Adriana had nothing else to say. In her mind, her

decision had already been made.

"So, you have two choices. It's either Botis or the blade," he said, extending his fist out and slowly loosening it.

As he opened his fist, the giant hand wrapped around her mimicked his action, relinquishing its death-grip to the sounds of her structure cracking. Adriana swiftly turned her gaze to Celeste who was still crying and gagging on the long worm as it continued to squirm and flail in her jowl.

"I'm sorry, I love you," she bellowed running to the brim of the platform and suicide diving over.

Her fear-stricken cries could be heard for minutes and minutes. Psycho and Celeste sat there taking it in before he looked back over to her.

"Okay, so it looks like I forgot an option. Honestly, I don't think you wanna go that way, most people will die of terror before they actually reach the pit and if you do somehow reach it, well, let's just say you'll wish you hadn't," Psycho explained while unclenching his other fist and releasing the grip upon her.

Her worm still hadn't made its way completely down her throat. It still sat wriggling relentlessly while her mouth ached like she'd never known to be possible.

"I don't understand why you guys won't just roll the dice with Botis; it might not be so bad."

She had a feeling it was much worse, much, much worse than she could imagine. But then again, the whole point of being young was exploring your curiosities. As horrified as she was, she was seeing something that almost no one else probably ever would. Something that was a privilege, no matter how nefarious.

"What the hell?" she thought.

Celeste raised her heavy skull up and squinted before trudging forward and beginning her lengthy ascension up the demonic staircase. As her tired foot took its first step, all she could think of was that there was no college on earth that could have ever given her this experience.

ORIGINAL COVER ART

ABOUT THE AUTHOR

Aron lives in Rhode Island with his fantastic soon to be wife, Katie. In his free time, he works on disturbing books and the Evil Examined Podcast and website. Aron is a failed musician but made a fairly sizable catalog of music that was about the same tone as his writing. He has always been a fan of horror and pushing to a new extreme. When he's not writing about the savage, degenerate thoughts trapped in his mind, he's reading 50s EC Comics, watching the most disturbing forgotten splatter movies, or The Twilight Zone.

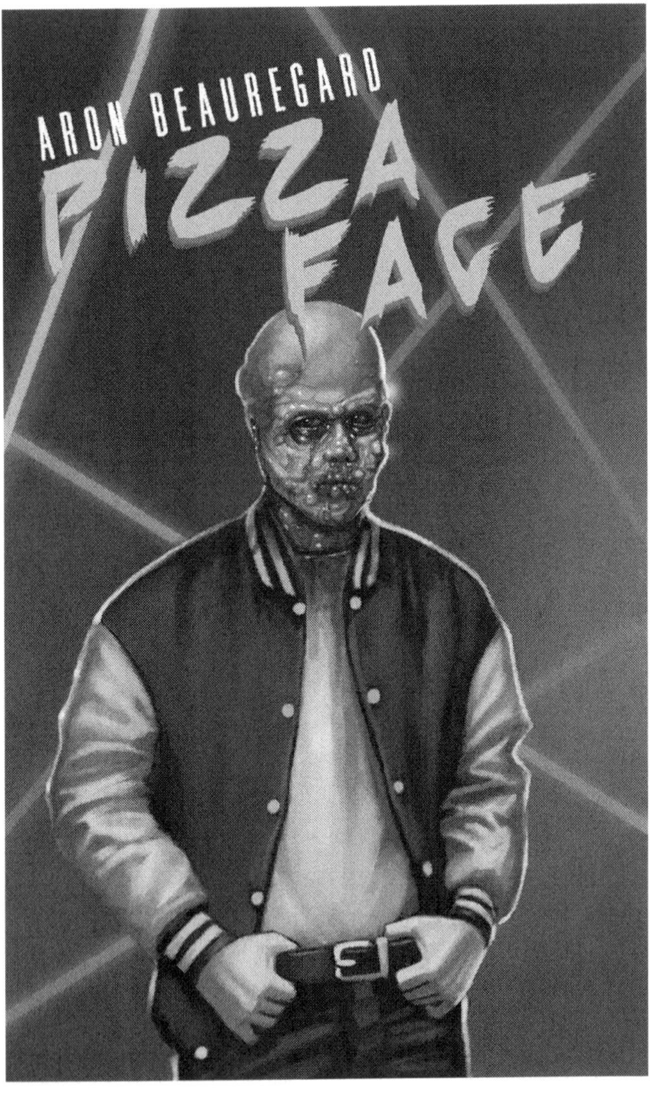
ARON BEAUREGARD
PIZZA FACE

GET YOUR SLICE OF THE PIE
BEFORE EVERYONE DIES!

What if you were the cock of the walk in high school? Worshipped by all for your flawless appearance and arrogant persona, until you woke up one morning to find that your once pristine skin had been stolen and replaced with a pus-oozing, malformed flesh-scape? What if shadows were given a will of their own? What if the family dog stumbled upon a new class of bizarre and highly aggressive animals?

What if there was a way to still physically be with a loved one after they passed on? What if the plants around us found a different kind of solace in the affection we display?

Find out the answers in Pizza Face.

ORIGINAL, HAND-DRAWN VILE WORKS
OF ART INCLUDED

SOME STAINS DO NOT COME OUT...

Raised in a household that was so filthy, it was stomach spilling, Vera has become a neat-freak. Her obsession with cleanliness sprouts the concept that her skills can be put to use in a unique way. In an effort to generate some income for her and her disabled husband, Daniel, just prior to the birth of their first child, she takes aim at the booming door to door sales business of the late 80s. All is going well until she arrives at the steps of a house she wished she never had. The steps of an evil that brings back the ghastly memories she so desperately tried to wash away.

Nothing will prepare you for the nastiness, disorder, and uncleansable horror brought forth by... The Slob.

ORIGINAL, HAND-DRAWN HORRIFYING WORKS OF ART INCLUDED

THIS HALLOWEEN THE SANITARIUM DOORS HAVE OPENED
FOR SPINE-TINGLING SAMHAIN SLAUGHTER!

SCARY BASTARD

ARON BEAUREGARD

BONES CRUSHED, PULLED OUT GUTS, CANDY AND HOMICIDAL NUTS!

What do a brilliant child killer, a hopeful special effects artist, a duo of budding teen spree killers, a student-screwing teacher, and a mutated maniac with his lower jaw missing have in common?

They're all out this Halloween.

How will their paths cross? Who will be butchered? Can anyone survive this bloodbath or are they all destined to drown in a pool of warm red? This slasher nightmare gives you a seat right beside the killer but don't get too comfortable, there's a Scary Bastard on the loose...

ORIGINAL, HAND-DRAWN HIDEOUS WORKS OF ART INCLUDED

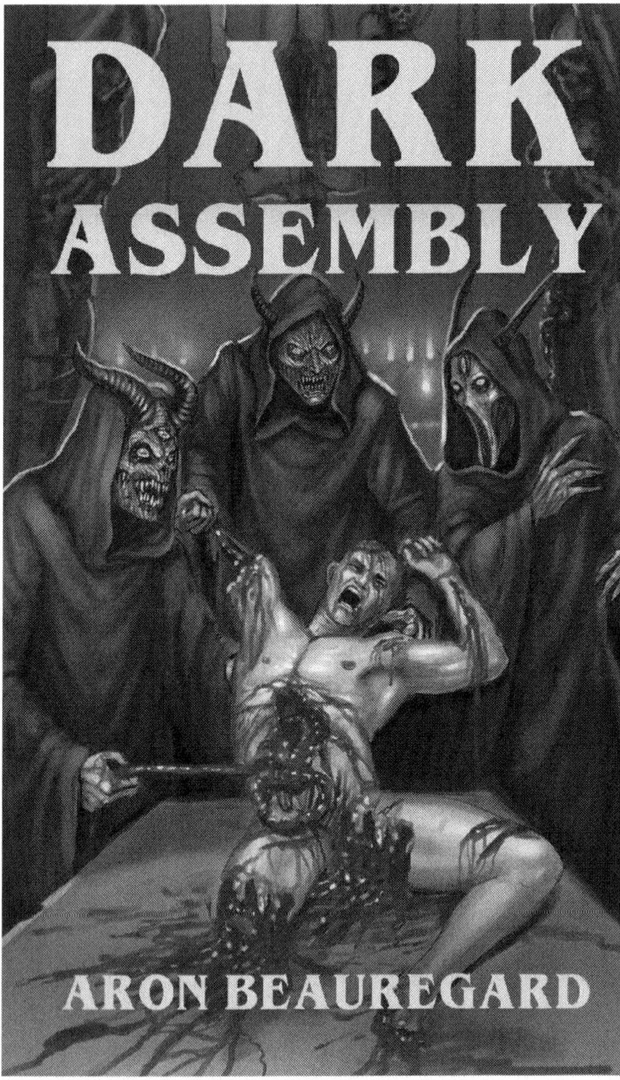
DARK
ASSEMBLY
ARON BEAUREGARD

TAKE PRIDE IN YOUR DYSFUNCTION

This assembly of putrid tales will drag you into the darkest regions of humanity. It will push extremes and test the mental moral boundaries of those who choose to participate. Meet a woman who carries a dead baby in her womb that she believes will somehow find life again. Join two teenage psychopaths as they bring hell to the suburbs on Devil's Night. Follow a child of the streets that finally steered away from a life of crime, only to be drawn back by a bizarre new drug. Take part in a gruesome and nefarious ritual that can restore one's innocence, or worm your way into the dark web beside a sadistic pedophile with a bottomless desire to kill and fuck.

How should you feel after digesting these admittedly obscene and repulsive stories? Ask yourself if enjoying them makes you a horrible person or if hating them somehow justifies your journey into this storm of violence and perversion. For the sick and willing, please join in our Dark Assembly...

INCLUDES 20 REPULSIVE, HAND-DRAWN ABOMINATIONS

Made in the USA
Coppell, TX
14 December 2023